Talayah & Yasir

Talayah

It was approximately five-thirty pm when I got home from work and as soon as I entered my apartment, I got irritated.

"Why is it that every time I come home, you're in the same spot that I left you in?" I asked my live-in boyfriend, Antonio. He let out an annoyed sigh, quickly glanced at me then rolled his eyes. I started to snap just for the simple fact that he had an attitude as if he was the one that had been out working all day.

"You just got home and you already starting with me?" he asked, casually flicking through the channels. If looks could kill Antonio would be taking his last breath right now. I was so tired of going through the same old thing with him. It felt like every single day was on a constant loop, the same thing happening over and over again.

"I'm starting with you because I've been gone for the past twelve hours and yo ass is still in this same damn spot! You don't see an issue with that?" I questioned placing my purse on the end table. I walked over to the TV and stood in front of it, blocking his view of the game displayed on the screen. I folded my arms under my breast and gave him a look. Antonio sucked his teeth and rubbed his hand over his face.

"Lay move. Ain't nobody in the mood for this shit man," he said in an annoyed tone.

"Get your bum ass up Antonio! Damn! Every day I gotta come home and scream at you like you're a little kid. You're a grown ass man living up under your girlfriend's roof. You're not contributing to these bills, cooking, cleaning, or doing anything productive. You just sit on that couch everyday feeling sorry for yourself. Get over it! No man is supposed to be living off of his

2

woman. A man is supposed to be a protector. You ain't protecting shit. All you do is sit in this house, and when you're not in the house you're God knows where doing God knows what with God knows who. I'm tired of it! You need to get your shit together. I'm not built to take care of somebody's son. Especially when they're living with me rent free and out here dogging me out every chance they get! If you want somebody to coddle you, go back to ya Mama's house. I'm not the one," I said finally letting out all my frustrations. I kept so much bottled up for the sake of preventing an argument or getting my ass beat, but I had time today. Antonio looked up at me like I had lost my mind.

"Who the fuck you think you talkin to?" he asked raising his voice. He grabbed the remote to cut the TV off and stood up moving closer to me. We were so close that we could kiss. As stupid as it probably sounded, I wanted to. I would never admit it, but I was both intimidated and turned on by his height and muscles. I was only 5'5", so his 6'5" two-hundred something-pound body towered over me. Not only was he a lot larger than I was, I also knew how his temper could be. I wouldn't be surprised if he choked me up and tossed me all around this living room. It wouldn't be the first time.

I guess in a sick twisted way, I enjoyed the disfunction, which is probably why I haven't left his disrespectful ass yet. He would cheat on me, hit me or talk to me crazy and I'd be done, but then as soon as I was ready to leave him, he'd do something to pull me back in. Like I said, our relationship was on a constant loop and I battled with myself every day to stick it out or leave him.

Even though I loved him, I had to admit that my patience was growing very thin with this man. I wanted him to either do right or leave me the fuck alone. I stared into his brown eyes and resisted the urge to kiss him.

Antonio Kamar James was fine as hell, and he always had been. He had milk chocolate skin, full pink lips, a full beard and a curly high-top fade. At first, I hated the cut, but it started to grow on me.

He was my baby, my high school sweetheart and I was well

aware of the fact that things between us had changed drastically, but I still tried to make it work just for the sake of me having "the love of my life". I honestly wasn't sure if I could give him that title and mean it. I know I loved him, but I don't think I was in love with him anymore. After so many lies, arguments, cheating and disrespect, I eventually fell out of love with him. That should have been a red flag right there, but I ignored it, much like I ignored everything that was wrong with our relationship. I guess because I've loved him for so long, I didn't want to feel like I wasted all these years. I had to have something to show for it.

"I wish that you would just chill out and ride with me while I'm going through this storm. You don't know how to be supportive at all. Tell me it's going to be okay, let me know that you got me no matter what. You don't do any of that and you expect me to wanna do better and do right by you. Fuck out of here," he said waving his hand dismissively and brushing past me. As he brushed past, his shoulder roughly bumped mine. I rolled my eyes and watched as he disappeared down the hallway.

Even after he'd been out of the room for a few moments, I stood frozen in place. I wanted to move, but I couldn't. I was still processing what he'd just said to me. *What does he mean I'm not supportive? I've been supporting him by providing a roof over his head,* I thought to myself. I almost let myself feel bad, but quickly snapped out of it as I made my way towards the bedroom where Antonio was.

"SUPPORTIVE?! You wanna talk about supportive? Nigga I've been supporting ya broke ass since you lost your job, the fuck you mean? It's been a year Antonio and you haven't done a damn thing but allow me to take care of everything around here. You don't put in on shit, you drive my car like it's yours, but never come back with anything but this fucking attitude; complaining and disrespecting me like you really out here doing what you need to do. Don't try to make me feel bad because I want you to do better. That's what a real one does. Anybody who gives a fuck about you would tell you that," I said folding my arms under my breasts again. I had pitied him and allowed him to sulk for the first three months, but now things were getting out of hand.

Almost a year ago, one of Antonio's female co-workers, April began flirting with him and making sexual advances. Based on what he told me, April was an attractive Caucasian woman, but Antonio just wasn't interested. Not because he was too faithful to cheat, but because his career would be on the line. A month went by, and April's advances had only gotten worse. She'd gone from subtly flirting to showing up half naked in his office and sending him sexual pictures via their work e-mail.

When Antonio brought the issue to me, I suggested that he take it to his human resources department and file a sexual harassment case. Antonio didn't think it was that serious and took matters into his own hands. He'd wanted me to get riled up, threaten to whoop her ass, cuss her out or do something out of my character. However, he didn't get any of that. I gave him the politically correct answer since he claimed he wanted to handle the situation in the right way. He wanted me to be his "ride or die," in that moment, but I refused. He got irritated by what he thought was lack of support, and stupidly sent a nasty e-mail to April letting her know that he did not want her, and that she needed to leave him alone. He even went as far as confronting her in the work place and choking her up, which April took as a sign that he wanted her. Yes, you heard right. The bitch is sick in the head.

Once he made it clear that they would never be together, April became angry. She was hurt by his rejection and as revenge, went to HR and told management that he had been harassing her. Without even asking for proof, management immediately took her side and threatened to fire him. Before they could get the chance, he quit, and he'd been depressed about it ever since.

Antonio rubbed his hand over his face in frustration. He got off the bed and started packing a bag. He should have been making peace with his woman but instead he was getting ready to run away from his issues, as usual. Instead of responding to him, I sucked my teeth and walked out of the room towards the living room. I sat down on the couch and immediately, my mind began to race as I thought of every possible way I could either kick him out of the house or kill him.

I'd been with Antonio since I was seventeen years old, and there was a time when I thought we'd be together forever; however, the past two years had shown me a side of Antonio that I decided I didn't want to be with. I realized that we've just outgrown each other, but still, I couldn't just walk away from him, which was sad. I had all these things going for myself but here I was, being stupid. I allowed myself to be stuck with a man that I knew was cheating and disrespecting me on a regular basis.

At just twenty-six years old I was on my shit. I was drop dead gorgeous, standing at a mere 5'2", dark chocolate skin, big brown eyes, full plump lips, and a petite frame with curves in all the right places and long curly jet-black hair that was a hundred percent mine.

Not only was I one of the baddest females that I knew, I was a self-made boss. I was killing the hair and make-up game in Michigan and all over the US. I had always had a knack for styling hair and applying make-up. At sixteen, I'd started doing my friends and family's hair in my mother's basement for a small fee. When word got out that I could do hair, my client list started to build. I started seeing girls from my neighborhood and kids from schools close by. After six months, I was receiving too many clients to continue doing hair in a basement, so I attempted to rent a booth in a neighborhood salon. However, the owners of the salons I visited refused to offer me a booth until I got my cosmetology license.

While the majority of my high school class graduated and went off to college, I took a different route and went to school to get my license and the rest was history. Now, at the age of twenty-six, I own a shop that I call *"Black Girl Magic,"* housing the hottest hair and nail stylist, lash technicians, microbladers,, and make-up artist. I now have a huge client list, including local and national celebrities as well as my regulars that I've held for years.

At the same time that my career took off, my relationship with Antonio took a dive. It seemed as if Antonio was jealous of my new-found success, even before he quit his job. When I first opened *Black Girl Magic,* he was so supportive and proud of me. As I started to build a celebrity clientele and gain recognition around the city and state as a local celebrity, he started to be known as Talayah's man instead of just Antonio.

When I started to make a name for myself, he lashed out in the worst way. He would talk to me as if I was beneath him, making me feel like I wasn't worthy of all the hard work I put in, and made it seem like I needed him. To get away from the negative energy at home, I started coming in a little later than usual and Antonio acted as if I was out messing around instead of working. There had been a few nights that Antonio had put his hands on me in a fit of rage. Although I would fight back, I was really no match for him. I quickly realized that he was trying to break my spirit and I refused, but again, I couldn't walk away. I was disappointed in myself to say the least.

My thoughts were interrupted when I noticed Antonio enter the living room and head to the front door with a Nike bag. I watched him walk towards the dining room and grab my car keys off of the end table and continue towards the front door.

"Where do you think you're going with my car?!" I shouted hopping off of the couch.

"What you mean where I'm going? I'm about to leave out and let you have your space," he said in a calm tone.

"You can leave all you want to but you ain't going nowhere in my car. Give me my keys," I said holding my hand out.

"Man watch out," he said trying to push me out the way. I stumbled a bit, and out of reflex I cocked my arm back and smacked him in the face. He looked at me like he wanted to beat my ass but decided not to. For that, I was grateful. I really didn't feel like fighting with him tonight. He took two steps back and threw the keys at me.

"Take these keys before I really whoop yo ass Lay. I'll be back when I come back," he said and then walked out of the door. I didn't know where he was going or how he was getting there, and I damn near didn't care. I was going to enjoy his absence for however long he was going to be gone. Maybe when he came back,

I'll have my mind made up, or he'll realize how wrong he was and change. Wishful thinking.

Antonio

I was fuming as I waited for my Uber to pull up. Talayah brought out a side of me that I didn't like, but it seemed like she loved to push me. She was always hollering about me doing right by her, but she nagged so much that I didn't even want to do right. I used to, but after a while, I just said fuck it. Even when I was doing right, she accused me. So instead of being accused of some shit I wasn't doing, I went out and did my thing, that way her nagging and screaming wouldn't be in vain.

It seemed like no matter what I did, I was never going to be good enough for her. Even before I quit my job, I could tell that Talayah was giving up or just not in love with me anymore. I could be wrong, but I doubted it. I knew that girl like the back of my hand.

On the same token, I knew that I played a huge part in the reason why she'd been distant and bitter, but fuck all of that. She had to learn how to be the woman that I needed before I was going to want to become the man she wanted. I was the man and I demanded to be respected as one. If I felt that the respect was fading away, I would do what I needed to prove to her, and myself, that I was still the one in charge, even if it meant whooping her ass when I need to.

Yes, I cheated, lied, and just plain old abused Lay over the years. I knew that Talayah didn't trust me one bit, and was probably terrified of me most times, but I was never going to stop doing what I wanted to do. My father and mother stayed married for thirty-five years before he passed away and they were the happiest couple I knew. I grew up watching him slap my Mom around and cheat on her with women he would tell me were my "Aunties," but I knew he loved my Mom and she knew it too. That was the reason why she never left. The love kept them together. At least that's what I thought.

I needed a real ride or die like my Mama, and I still think that's Talayah, but she gives up so easily. So, until she acts right, I'm going to continue to do my thing. Even when she does get it together, I'll probably still keep one or two on the side for when Lay is on my nerves. That's just how I was wired.

My Uber finally pulled up and I hopped in, ready to get to my destination. We drove for a few miles before pulling up to my favorite hole in the wall bar and grill called Zino's. It almost looked like an abandoned building, but the people that lived around here knew better. Zino's had the strongest drinks and the best soul food that I've ever had. Whenever I felt down, I would drown my sorrows here, and often times have a one-night stand with the baddest female I could find. There was no better way for a man to get his mind off of things than some strong liquor, good food, and tight pussy.

I stepped out of the car and made my way to the bar. As soon as I opened the door the scent of chicken frying filled my nostrils. I smirked as I walked through the door and headed towards the bar to take a seat. It only took a few moments for a bartender to come over to me.

"Your usual Tony?" she asked. I looked at her and nodded my head. I watched her ass jiggle from left to right with each step she took. *Damn,* I thought. I'd always wanted to get closer to her, but every time I came into the bar, she curved me like I was a lame nigga. I didn't care though; I wanted her badly and I was going to get her eventually. She was bad as hell without even knowing it. She had caramel skin, short black hair that touched her shoulders, deep dimples, white teeth, and amber eyes that held a hint of darkness. I wanted to fuck of course, but I also kind of wanted to know more about her. She wasn't having it though.

As much as I hate to admit it, my ego was a little bruised every time she turned me down. I wasn't used to rejection. I knew that I was an attractive man and I could have any woman that I wanted. Why would one turn me down?

I watched as she headed towards me with my drink in her hand. She sat the drink down in front of me and attempted to walk away from me, but I grabbed her arm. Immediately, she snatched away from me and gave me a look that made me hold my hands up in mock surrender.

"Don't fucking touch me," she said through gritted teeth.

"Damn, what I do to you?" I asked.

"I'm not interested. I would have thought you'd get the hint by now, but you keep trying. Leave me the hell alone," she said with an attitude and then walked away, switching. I shook my head and chugged my double shot of Hennessy. She could play hard to get all she wanted, but if I didn't know anything else, I knew how to read a bitch. She wanted me, she just didn't want to admit it.

Three double shots later, I was feeling pretty good. The bar was dead, but I had a couple of hoes on speed dial I knew I could call for times like this. The pretty bartender had finished her shift and left without looking my way. I started to go after her, but I didn't want to hound her. Instead, I pulled out my phone to order another Uber and then I dialed a number.

"Yeah?" the sultry voice answered.

"You at home?" I asked.

"Yeah, come on," she said and then hung up. That's what I liked; short, sweet and straight to the point. I paid my tab and then headed outside to wait for my Uber to take me to my destination. *Hopefully this bitch doesn't get on my nerves so I can chill for a couple of days*, I thought. One thing about the girls that I chose, they always had some smart-ass mouths and terrible ass attitudes, but all of that made me more attracted to them.

Talayah

"So, what are you going to do?" my best friend Giselle asked me. We were having lunch at our favorite crab place, *Detroit Pho & Crab,* sharing a bucket of crab legs, crawfish, corn, and potatoes. We were greedy to say the least. Food was pretty much the foundation of our friendship.

"I don't know. I just need to figure out a way to get him the hell out of my house and out of this relationship. It's going to take more than me saying I don't want to be with him. I don't think he'll let me leave willingly. He's been in a depressed funk and I tried to be understanding, but the boy has a degree, G. It's not like he can't take his talents elsewhere. I'm just so tired of the up and down. Anytime I threaten to kick him out or leave he magically starts to act right, but it only last for so long. He gets comfortable again and then it's back to the same old shit," I said stuffing a potato in my mouth and rolling my eyes. I didn't really feel like talking about my failing relationship, but Giselle is the only person that I can vent to without being judged or feeling like a dumbass.

"Do you hear yourself? You just said he won't let you leave like that nigga is holding you hostage or some shit. You know whenever you're ready, I have Beanie on speed dial, or we can always slash his tires, pour sugar in his tank or put poison in his food. Whatever you wanna do," she said shrugging and sucking the head of a crawfish. I looked at my friend and laughed at her crazy comment. Giselle had always been blunt like this. She spoke her mind no matter what came out or who it offended. Not only was she outspoken, but she had the hands to back it up. I could count on both hands how many times we had to fight a group of females because of Giselle's mouth; but no matter what, we were best friends, and had been since we were five years old. Blood couldn't make us any closer.

"I know, but I don't think it needs to come to that just yet. Once Beanie finds out it won't be no stopping him and I don't think I'm ready for all that drama. I'll figure something out on my own. Maybe I should just find another spot and let him have that apartment. Find a way to take my name off the lease, put his name on it and then leave," I said, and Giselle nodded her head.

Beanie was Giselle's older brother, who also happened to be a well-known rapper in not only the city of Detroit but in the state of Michigan and other parts of the United States. Beanie ran with a group that went by the name D-Boyz, and they were responsible for a lot of murders that went on in the city. Beanie and I were super close, almost like brother and sister. We used to have a small crush on each other at one point, but it quickly faded once I became "part of the family," I knew he wouldn't hesitate to handle Antonio for me if need be, but I wasn't ready for the man to die. I just wanted him to get his shit together.

"You could do that. But how are you going to get him to sign the papers to transfer the lease in his name?" Giselle asked snapping me out of my thoughts.

"That'll be the easy part. All I have to do is fill him up with food, liquor and some pussy, he'll do whatever I want him to do in the heat of the moment," I said smirking. Men were easy to please and manipulate.

"You nasty," Giselle said playfully, and we laughed.

"So, what's been up with you? I haven't seen you in weeks," I said changing the subject. I was tired of talking about my love life.

"Girl, work has been keeping me on my toes, but I love it so far," she said smiling from ear to ear, causing me to smile. Giselle had recently snagged a job with the local news as a lead anchor for the nightly news. She'd always wanted to be an anchor, sitting behind that desk and in front of the camera. She was born for it.

"I'm so proud of you and thank you for suggesting that they hire me as your personal hair & makeup artist," I said, and Giselle waved her hand.

"Girl of course. Those white mothafuckas don't know how to slay me like you. I wish I would let them fuck up all this hard work we've put in," she said playing with her hair and giggling. We finished eating, paid for the food and then got up from the booth that we were sitting in. Just as we were exiting the restaurant a small group of men walked in, one of them damn near knocking me over.

"Watch where you're going!" I said in an irritated tone. I looked up and my words almost got caught in my throat as I looked in the eyes of one of the finest man I'd ever seen. He had smooth chocolate skin, dark eyes that seemed to look straight through me and a full beard. As I looked him up and down, I was impressed with his style, which was pretty laid back. He was dressed casually in an all-black Nike jogger set and black Timberland boots. A single white gold Cuban link chain rested on his neck and a white gold watch that I couldn't get a good look at sat on his wrist. His vibe screamed out drug dealer or scammer but that didn't stop me from gawking at him. It was something about his aura that captivated me, and he hadn't even said a word.

"My bad baby, I didn't mean to run into you like that," he said in a deep, silky voice that could take the panties right off of a woman. I attempted to subtly smooth out my hair with my hand while I thought of something to say. I didn't want him to know that I was at a loss for words. I wanted to come off as if I wasn't fazed by his fine ass.

"Don't worry about it. Just be more careful," I said trying my best to portray an attitude. I was just about to walk away, but he lightly grabbed me arm. I gave him a look that said, *"why the hell are you touching me,"* which caused him to let go of the slight grip that he had on me. Honestly speaking, his soft hands felt good on my skin, even if only for half of a second.

"Before you leave, can I ask your name?" he asked politely.

"Talayah," I said. He stuck his hand out for me to shake, which I did.

"Yasir," he said smiling, showcasing his perfect white teeth. I had to use all of my strength to keep my knees from buckling.

The man was damn near perfect.

"Nice to meet you," I said casually.

"You as well. I don't want to seem too forward, but I would really like to get to know you. Can I take down your number?" he asked. The question caught me off guard, although it shouldn't have. Men flirted with me every day, but then again this wasn't any man. There wasn't a man alive that could stop me in my tracks the way that Yasir had just done and it made me nervous. I was used to always being in control.

"I'm sorry, I have a man," I said, remaining loyal to the man I had waiting at home. I heard Giselle suck her teeth behind me. I looked back and gave her a look to tell her to stop it, but Giselle just shrugged her shoulders as if she was telling me she didn't give a fuck. *I should just give him my number, Antonio won't be around for too much longer anyway*, I thought to myself.

"Damn, well, don't take this in the wrong way, but I hope he fucks up soon, and I hope I run into you again after he does," he said to me, never breaking eye contact. "Have a great day ladies," he said speaking to both of us, then walked off to find the people that he walked in with. I stayed frozen in place, watching him walk away.

"You could've at least taken his number. That man was fine as hell. You don't just randomly meet fine men like that every day," Giselle rambled as we headed towards our cars.

"I wouldn't have felt right. No matter how bad I may have wanted to give him my number, I just can't allow myself to do it when I know I'm in a whole relationship," Talayah sighed.

"Girl, bye. I would have given him my number, went home and kicked Antonio's ass out. You deserve more than what he's been giving you Lay-Lay and you know it. You don't have to settle for less just because you love him, and you've been with him for a long time. You don't owe that man anything and he's definitely not worth your happiness. But, it's your life and I won't be that friend that's encouraging you to leave your man. If you're happy, I'm happy. I will say this though, if he puts his hands on you again, I'm calling Beanie and it's nothing you can do to stop me," she said in a serious tone. I looked at my best friend and held my hands up in mock surrender.

"Okay, okay," I said opening the driver's side door of my car. "Call or text me when you get home," I said, and Giselle nodded getting into her car. As I got into my own car and started up the engine, my mind wandered to the fine stranger that I'd met just a few minutes ago. *If it's meant for him to be around, I'll run into him again.*

I was halfway to my house when Antonio called me. Begrudgingly, I answered the phone. He had just gotten back to the apartment yesterday, after being gone for two days. He'd been on his "best behavior.", but I still wasn't really feeling him. I knew this act would only last for so long.

"Yeah?"

"Where are you?" he asked.

"On my way to the house. I'm about five to ten minutes away," I said.

"Okay, hurry back. I have something for you," he said sounding excited.

"Something for me? What is it?" I asked.

"Now if I tell you, it wouldn't be a surprise. You'll see when you get here," he said causing me to smile. It had been so long since Antonio had done anything nice for me that I forgot how sweet and romantic he used to be.

"Okay, I'll see you in a minute," I said and then disconnected the call.

A few minutes later, I was walking through the door of my apartment, and immediately noticed how clean the house was. Everything was in its rightful place and it smelled like apple cinnamon, my favorite scent. *What is he up to?* I thought to myself.

"Antonio!" I called out. Seconds later, he appeared from the bedroom with a smirk on his face. He looked handsome, yet casual in a pair of black jeans an olive Nike pullover and olive-green Timberlands. *He always did look good in olive,* I thought to myself.

"Wassup baby," he greeted, walking up to me and kissing my cheek.

"What's all of this?" I asked referring to the house.

"I just wanted to show you that I'm really going to try and do better by you baby. I know I've been on some real fuck shit lately, and I know you're probably sick and tired of me, but you didn't give up on me, and I really appreciate you for that," he said to me. Looking in his eyes, he seemed genuine.

"I think we need to talk," I said ready to lay it all out on the table.

"We can, but first come in the bedroom. I want to show you something," he said trying to lead me to the bedroom.

"Are you tryna get some right now?" I asked. I know he wasn't trying to get in my panties after his ass was just out with some bitch. I didn't have proof that he was, but I knew Antonio. He looked back at me and laughed.

"Nah bae, just come here for a second," he said trying to lead me again. This time, I followed. When we entered the room, I half expected to see some sort of shopping or gift bag, but all I saw was a suit and tie laid out on the bed. Antonio looked at me with a wide smile, while I looked back at him, confused.

"You bought a new suit?" I asked, and he nodded. "For what?"

"I have an interview in the morning," he said, and I was a little taken aback.

"An interview? When did you even apply for a new position?" I asked.

"I've been applying for a while now. That's what you didn't know. You were so stuck up your own ass you never bothered to ask what I do when you're not here. All you see is me 'in the same spot,'" he said mocking me. I rolled my eyes. *Here we go*, I thought. I was going to respond with an attitude but decided against it. I didn't feel like having the same old argument.

"I'm sorry I doubted you. It just seemed like you weren't trying, but I'm happy to see that you are," I said, and Antonio nodded.

"Thanks."

"So, where's this interview? What company?" I asked,

genuinely interested.

"I'm interviewing at 3M Engineering as a mechanical engineer," he said, and I nodded my head.

"That's good. That's really good," I said. He was a mechanical engineer at his old job so this was right up his alley.

"I'm going to get back on my feet Lay and I'm going to be a better man not only for you but for myself. We both deserve it," he said grabbing my hands.

"Sit down really quick," I said taking a seat on the queen-size bed.

"What's wrong? I thought you'd be a little more excited," he said with a look of disappointment.

"I'm very happy for you, I really am, but I need to seriously talk about us. I don't want this to be just another twist and turn on this rollercoaster you got me on. We need to be on the same page, or we just don't need to be together," I said in a calm yet stern tone.

"Man, what are you talking about?" he questioned. I could see on his face that he was getting irritated, but I didn't care.

"I'm talking about this same old pattern that we keep going through. Yeah, your attitude has improved and you're taking steps towards bettering yourself, and I appreciate that, but I can't help but wonder if you're only doing this because I threatened to kick you out. I mean it's only been a few days since you walked out Antonio. You do this every time you think I'm going to leave, then when you think we're in a comfortable place again, you show your ass. I'm sick and tired of the disrespect and the abuse. Either you're going to commit to being a better man or I'm done, and I mean that. I'm not taking the same shit from you over and over. I've given you more than enough chances this past year, you don't have any more with me," I said finally putting my foot down.

No matter how mad he got, I felt a sense of relief finally getting that off of my chest. I was prepared for the remainder of the conversation to take a turn for the worst. Antonio remained silent for at least sixty seconds. My hands were starting to sweat, waiting for him to fly off the handle.

"Look, I'm sorry for everything Lay-Lay. I really am. I'm

sorry for talking to you crazy and I'm sorry that I've gotten physical with you. You didn't deserve that & I know that. I'm going to do better, I promise," he said looking right into my eyes to let me know that he was serious. I wanted to believe him, but only time would tell. His words didn't really mean shit to me.

Antonio was well aware of what he had been doing to damage this relationship with me. Not just these past few months, but over the years. If it wasn't the females he messed around with, it was him verbally or physically abusing me. He never felt like he needed to change because I always took him back, even when I threatened to leave. I was serious this time though. He didn't have any more chances to treat me like I wasn't shit.

Antonio went on to tell me that he'd made a conscious decision just a couple of weeks ago that enough was enough and started to apply for jobs. He didn't tell me right away because he felt there was no use in celebrating until it actually happened. He'd even been on a few interviews, but hadn't gotten any offers, until now. He knew a few people working at 3M and had them put a word in for him. He'd spoken with the hiring manager and lead mechanic engineer, who'd offered him the position via FaceTime, so he knew he had the position in the bag. The interview was just a formality.

"Okay, we will see. I'm only trying if I see that you are. I'm going off of whatever vibe that I get from you. So, if I start acting funny, just know I'm following your lead," I said, and Antonio nodded his head. He could sense that I was losing faith in him, if I hadn't already. I don't think that anything could really make it better at this point. It was too late to try and fix it, but I was going to go along with the flow until I came up with a plan to get the hell out of this relationship.

Chapter Four

Antonio

The next day, I walked out of 3M feeling like a new man. I literally felt like I was on top of the world. I'd just finished filling out all the paperwork for 3M and was set to start on Monday, which was in four days. I was tempted to call my boys and have a few drinks to celebrate, but then I thought about Talayah. I'd told her that I was going to change for the better and I meant it. Pulling out my iPhone, I dialed her phone number and waited for her to pick up.

"You got it?" she asked, answering on the third ring. It made me smile to hear her sound so excited.

• •

"I just got done with the paperwork," I said getting into the car.

"I'm proud of you Ant," she said in a sincere tone. This was the first time she'd said something positive to me in a long time, so it meant a lot to hear this coming from her right now.

"Thanks bae. I was thinking that we could go out tonight to celebrate," I suggested.

"I wish I could, but I don't think I'm leaving the shop until ten tonight. I'm completely booked today," she said sighing. I rolled my eyes. I shouldn't have been irritated knowing that she was working, but I was.

"Alright don't worry about it," I said trying to mask my irritation.

"Don't get mad Antonio," she said, her tone matching mine.

"I ain't. It's straight," I said and then disconnected the call without even saying goodbye. I know I probably pissed her off by hanging up in her face, but I didn't care. If she didn't have time for me, I knew somebody that did. I quickly dialed my "next best thing".

"Why are you calling me?" La'Corsha, my on again off again side chick answered. Not only was she my side chick, she was my ex-girlfriend that I broke up with after I started dating Talayah. As much as I tried to stay away from her and do right by Talayah, I just couldn't. Especially when Talayah was too busy for me, which seemed to be more often than not.

"Man chill out. What you doing?" I asked, trying to figure out if she was at home or not.

"In my skin nigga, what do you want?" she asked with an attitude.

"Nothing man, damn," I said once again disconnecting the call. *These bitches out of control today.* All I wanted to do was celebrate my good news, and nobody was fucking with me. Annoyed, I started my car and pulled off. After driving for a few minutes, my phone rang. Without looking at the caller ID, I answered.

"Yeah?"

"Don't hang up in my face. I was just playing with you," La'Corsha said laughing. I sucked my teeth. I wasn't in a playful mood. I was pissed off at the fact that the person I really wanted to spend some time with wasn't trying to make an attempt to really get us back on track. She talked all that shit about me doing right by her, and putting forth some effort into this relationship, but she wasn't putting in any effort her damn self.

"Alright," I said in a dry tone.

"What's wrong with your crazy ass?" she asked trying to figure out why I wasn't in the mood to play around like I usually was.

"I just wanted to celebrate with Lay and she curved me," I said. I regretted even verbalizing my feelings the moment the words left out of my mouth. I knew I sounded like a punk. La'Corsha sucked her teeth before she responded.

"You can always come celebrate with me," La'Corsha said in an effort to pick me up. "We can do whatever you want." That last statement piqued my interest.

"Whatever I want huh?" I asked.

"Of course," she responded.

"Alright, bet. Give me about twenty minutes," I said before disconnecting the call. I guess something was better than nothing, right?

I stopped and got a family meal from Popeyes and then headed to LaCorsha's house. One thing about Co, she was simple. She didn't need a whole lot to make her happy and Popeyes would always make her happy.

I pulled up in front of her condo, killed the engine and sat in the car for a few minutes. For the first time in my life, I felt bad about being over here when I knew I shouldn't but fuck it. This is what happens when you leave your man lonely. I got out the car, grabbed the food and walked to her door. Right before I knocked on the front door, it swung open. La'Corsha greeted me in an oversized white t-shirt and black boy shorts. She didn't have any make up on her face and her hair was in a ponytail. I couldn't lie, she'd always been naturally beautiful. She always put me in the mind of a young Lisa Bonet, just a little thicker. One of the first things that attracted me to her was her long black curly hair. I don't know, why, but it always did something to me.

La'Corsha LeAnne Parkins had been in my life even before I knew Talayah. We'd basically grown up together and I had always had a crush on her, but she always friend zoned me. She even would go as far to tell people that we were cousins. I used to try and flirt with her, but she never got the hint. I guess after time passed, I wore her down and we dated. Things were going fine until I met someone else. That someone else being Talayah, and the rest was history.

La'Corsha fell back after I really started becoming serious with Talayah and we lost touch until she came back into my life a couple of years ago. I could tell that she still felt a way about me picking Talayah over her. She would throw out shady comments whenever I mentioned Talayah or just give off a jealous vibe. The two of them had never come in contact with one another and for that I was grateful. Talayah would probably kill me and LaCorsha if she found out we'd been fucking around all this time.

I still remember running into Co again. It was the first time I had ever cheated on Talayah and I'd been hooked ever since.

On my twenty-fourth birthday, Talayah and I got into a heated argument about a chick she'd caught me texting. It was honestly nothing going on between me and ole girl, but she wasn't trying to hear it. After about an hour of screaming and shouting, Lay stormed out of the house leaving me to celebrate my birthday alone. I called up a few of my boys and met them at this strip club called "The Pantheon," in Dearborn. Unbeknownst to me, La'Corsha was working there as a stripper and just so happened to be there that night. When I pulled up with my niggas, she was just getting on the stage. I didn't know who she was at first because she started her set with a mask on. By the time she took the mask off she was down to nothing but her G-String and stripper heels. When I realized who she was, my dick got hard as a rock. We made eye contact for a split second, but she quickly looked away. She was probably embarrassed, but she had no reason to be. I was completely turned on. I had literally dreamed about seeing this girl naked, and there she was in front of dozens of thirsty niggas, stripping for singles. I guess I was turned on and pissed off at the same time because I never got the chance to fuck while we were together.

Once she was done with her set, she quickly got off the stage and disappeared into the back of the building. I continued to watch the other strippers and even got a couple of drinks and lap dances before she came over to the booth that we were all sitting in. A couple of my niggas spoke to her, but she quickly ignored them and focused on me.

"Can I talk to you?" she asked, and I nodded my head. "In private," she said once she noticed I wasn't getting up. I nodded my head again before getting up and following her to one of the small private rooms the club had for the dancers to entertain "one on one".

"Wassup?" I asked once we entered the room.

"You must think I'm some kind of hoe or something now, huh?" she asked, and I gave her a look that let her know I was confused.

"What you mean?"

"Don't play dumb."

"I'm not playin'," I said, and she giggled.

23

"Never mind, forget I said anything," she said trying to walk past me and out the door. I quickly blocked her path.

"No, speak your mind. You think because you dancing I think less of you?" I asked looking at her. She was looking down at the ground with her arms folded under her breast. It took her a few moments before she nodded her head. "Man chill out. You still the same Co to me. Shit, if anything else you just made my dream come true," I said. Now it was her turn to look at me confused.

"Huh?" she asked.

"You know how many times I dreamed about seeing you naked?" I asked and she burst out laughing.

"You play too much," she said loosening up.

"I'm serious. You had my dick hard as hell a few minutes ago," I said eyeing her body from head to toe. If you ask me, she was the baddest thing in here. She was just the right amount of thick and skinny. A lot of strippers had too much ass, making it easy to tell that they'd had work done. These days, when you see a natural body, you have to appreciate it, because they're rare. Sad to say, but it's true.

"What about now?" she asked biting her bottom lip in a seductive manner.

"Aye, Co, you know I got a girl. I can't go down that route with you, no matter how bad I want to," I told her.

"So, you want to?" she said walking closer to me. I allowed her to back me up against the wall and her hand traveled down to the bulge in my pants. My dick stiffened at her touch and she smirked at me. I fucked for the first time in that private room and I've been fucking her ever since.

"Are you just gonna stand there and look crazy?" she asked snapping me out of my thoughts. I walked through the door and gave her a hug. She smelled like vanilla and sugar, almost like a sugar cookie. Judging from her attire, she'd just gotten out the shower. Once I made my way through the front door, I headed to her living room and made myself comfortable on the couch. She was right behind me, joining me on the couch a few seconds later.

"You got something to drink?" I asked her.

"Of course, I do. That's all you want to do? You don't wanna go out or nothing to celebrate?" she asked, and I nodded my head to say no.

"Naw, I just wanna chill, drink and eat. I don't need to do too much, it's just a job," I shrugged.

"Yeah but it's a job you've been wanting for a long time now. You should be proud that you finally got it," she said with a smile on her face.

"I am proud, but I just wanna relax."

"That's cool," she said and went into the kitchen to get my drink. A few moments later she appeared and handed me my favorite drink, henny and coke on the rocks. "You sure you don't want to celebrate?" she asked again.

"Naw I'm straight we can just chill," I told her, and she nodded her head.

"What? You actually wanna spend time with me and not fuck. The sky is falling," she said playfully, running over to the window, and looking up at the sky. We both laughed. That was one thing I loved about her, she was so silly. We could joke and play all day like some kids. With Lay, it was mostly business. I guess they just brought out different sides of me, and I loved both of them to death. I knew it was fucked up to say, but I would never stop fucking with either of them unless they decided to stop dealing with me. Until then I was going to have my cake and eat it too.
Chapter Five

Talayah

"Can you do it like this?" one of my clients asked, showing me a picture of the hairstyle that she wanted. The hairstyle was simple; a middle part with curls.

"Of course. You want the curls just like that or did you want me to freestyle?" I asked.

"If you can curl it just like that, I'd appreciate it," she said smiling, causing me to smile back.

"Of course. I got you," I said and then walked her over to the shampoo bowl so that I could start on her hair. A lot of salon owners hired people to wash and blow dry, but I wasn't about to spend the extra money when I could just do it myself.

I loved being in my shop. It got my mind off of any problems that I was having in my personal life and allowed me to do something that I loved in my own space. In the beginning, I was the only one working because I couldn't afford to hire anyone else. Once I started receiving too many clients to handle on my own, I hired two other hairstylist, London and Treasure to take my overflow. They now have their own client list and I've also added four other women: a nail tech by the name of Harmony, an eyebrow waxer named Kimani, a lash tech named Sarayah and Kree, the receptionist. I loved my team. We'd grown to become family the past few years. I appreciated their loyalty to my brand, and I admired their desire to create their own empire while still supporting me. It's hard to find genuine people these days, and I'm blessed to have staff that rides for me no matter what.

"So, what are you getting all dolled up for? What's the occasion?" I asked making small talk with her. Her face was beat to the god's, so I knew it had to be her birthday, anniversary, or something special going on today.

"It's my boyfriend's birthday today. I have a private dinner planned and I'm going to decorate his apartment really nice and romantic and then put it on him," she said, and we giggled in unison.

"I know that's right girl. Remind him why he got with you in the first place," I told her.

"It shouldn't take all of that. He should know what he has and act accordingly on a daily basis," Harmony chimed in, being nosy as usual. I rolled my eyes and then looked at her. Harmony was the baby of the group and I loved her, but she was the nosiest person I'd ever met in my life, and always wanted to be the center of attention. She had to be in the middle of a conversation, picture, or anything that she thought would make people notice her. Not to mention, she swore she was right about everything.

"Sometimes it's nice to treat your man. He shouldn't have to be the one always giving. That's not how a healthy relationship works," my client said in response to Harmony. Surprisingly, she didn't say anything else.

About an hour and a half later, I was finishing up on my client. When I was done putting my finishing touches on her hair, I spun her around so that she could take a look at herself in the mirror behind me. The look on her face when she saw her reflection was priceless. She looked like she was damn near in tears.

"Do you like it?" I asked, even though I already knew the answer.

"I freaking love it! Thank you so much!" she said pulling her phone out to take selfies. This is what I do it for. I loved to make women feel beautiful.

"No problem! Make sure you come back and see me, ok?"

"Of course! How much do I owe you?" she asked putting her phone back in her bag and retrieving her wallet.

"A hundred fifty." She handed me the money and I thanked her, then put the cash in my fanny pack that I kept on me while I was working. I took the cape off of her and she got out of the chair at the same time that the door chimed, indicating that someone had walked in. I turned around to clean up my station and get ready for my next client.

"Hey baby, you're right on time," I heard my client say. I turned around, curious to see who this man was that had this woman wanting to do the most for him. When I looked up and noticed who it was, I almost peed on myself. I watched as he pecked her on the lips and for some reason, I felt jealous.

"You look good," he said, and she smiled from ear to ear.

"Thank you, baby, Talayah hooked me up," she said pointing to me. He looked at me and for half a second, he looked surprised then smirked.

"Thanks for getting my girl together," he said to me, putting emphasis on "my girl,"

"Anytime," I said and watched as they walked out. As they were walking out the door, my next client was walking in.

"Hey Lay!" she said waving at me.

"Hey boo. Give me just a second, I'll be ready for you, ok?"

"Go ahead, take your time," she said, and I hurried to the back towards my office. I shouldn't be feeling the way I am about a man that I don't even know. Why am I mad? Why am I jealous? I shouldn't be feeling any type of way about anybody else except the man I had at home. I quickly pulled out my phone and dialed the one person that can calm me down.

"Wassup hoe?" Giselle answered.

"Bitch! You'll never guess what happened."

"What?"

"You remember that dude we met about a week or so ago at Detroit Pho & Crab?" I asked.

"Yeah I remember his fine ass and I remember how you curved him too," she said, and I rolled my eyes.

"Well, he was just in my shop a few minutes ago, picking up his girl," I told her.

"Shut the fuck up!!" she screamed. I had to pull the phone away from my ear because she was so loud.

"I'm dead ass serious. And the kicker is, I just did his girlfriend's hair," I said slouching in my office chair.

"Ain't that some shit! And to think he was talking all that getting to know you mess, whole time he has a girlfriend. Niggas ain't shit," she said, and I shook my head.

"Why am I jealous though? As soon as I laid eyes on him, I got upset. I don't know that man from a can of paint. I don't have a reason to be upset, right?" I asked for clarification.

"No, you don't, but you probably wished you were her for a split second, but don't trip. You don't know what kind of hell he gives her behind closed doors," she stated, and I knew she was right. This is why I called Giselle. She always spoke nothing but facts.

"Yeah, you right," I said.

"I know I'm right. Now get off my phone and go back to work. Calling me mad about a nigga you don't even know. Girl please," she said and then disconnected the call. I chuckled, put my phone back in my pocket and headed out of my office to get back to work.

The rest of my day went by smoothly, but my mind kept wandering back to Yasir's fine ass. At this point, I was starting to feel like I was sick in the head for lusting after another woman's man, but I couldn't help it.

I quickly finished with my last clients. By the time I was finished with my last client, everyone had gone home, except Kree who was always the last to leave after tidying up and closing down the shop for me. I looked at my phone and saw that it was almost eight pm. I half expected a text or phone call from Antonio, but I didn't have either.

"Alright Kree, I'm heading out," I called out to her before heading towards the back door.

"Okay boss lady, be safe."

"You too," I said. I walked out of the door and into the parking lot, scrolling through social media. I was so wrapped up in my phone that I didn't even notice the tall figure leaning against the car parked next to mine. Finally, I looked up to unlock the doors on my car. I damn near jumped out of my skin once I noticed the figure standing a few feet away from me.

"You really need to pay attention to your surroundings this late at night. You talked about me watching where I was going, now look at you," the figure said in that silky voice that I'd heard before. I stood frozen in place, and I'm sure he picked up on it because he took a few steps towards me. "You and all that mouth don't have anything to say?" he asked now just a few feet away from me.

"Yasir, right?" I asked trying to play dumb.

"You remember my name Talayah, don't even do that," he said in a stern voice.

"What are you doing here?" I asked completely ignoring his last statement.

"I wanted to see if I could catch up with you," he said.

"Why? Shouldn't you be enjoying your girlfriend & your birthday right now?" I asked. He looked a little shocked at what I'd said.

"How'd you know it was my birthday?" he asked, and I gave him a look that said, "how else," and he nodded his head to show that he understood what I mean. "That ain't my girl either," he added.

"Yeah, great way to throw that in there after you've had time to think of a good lie. You literally thanked me for getting your girl together," I said with an attitude, putting emphasis on your girl. I walked past him and headed to my car.

"What you mad for?" he asked taking a step to the left, blocking me from getting to the door.

"I'm not mad, can you please move out of my way. You're super pressed right now. That's not cute," I told him. I used my arm to try and push him out the way, and instantly wished I hadn't. I don't know why I didn't expect him to be fit, but the boy was definitely built like a personal trainer. I could tell that just by briefly touching his chest.

"I'm not pressed about shit. I just know that we want – scratch that, I know that we need one another. You can keep trying to deny it by throwing in my face that you have a man, but we both know the real. Once you stop trying to fight it and get to know me, you'll realize I was right. I got what you need, and you got what I need. I don't care if we don't know each other like that. We have a connection; I feel it and I know you do too. But I'm not about to force you into it. You have to want me on your own," he said taking a step back. He turned to walk away but then stopped like he was thinking about something and turned back around to face me. "Give me your phone," he said.

"For what?" I asked, once again with an attitude.

"You ain't got to. Just remember (586) 223-7833," he said and then walked away. *Cocky ass* I thought as I got into my car. Is it bad that I liked that shit? Yeah, it's bad, I know. I got in the car and hurried to plug his number in my phone before I forgot it. I know, I'm not shit, don't remind me.

Chapter Six

Yasir

I wanted Talayah's sexy ass and I wanted her bad. I knew from the moment that I laid eyes on her that she's who I'm supposed to be with. She's so stuck on her bitch ass boyfriend that she can't recognize a real nigga right in her face. It didn't help that Renae was running her mouth in the shop about me. I guess it wasn't really her fault. She didn't know that I had my eyes on Talayah, and Talayah didn't know that I was involved with someone. All I know is that we both needed to get rid of who we're currently dealing with, but I can't force a grown ass woman to be with me. That's not the type of nigga that I am.

I got into my car and pulled off in the direction of my condo. I didn't even want to go out or do shit for my birthday, but Renae insisted that we did it big for my twenty-eighth birthday. Twenty-eight wasn't really a big deal, it was just another year for me to level up and make bands.

I pulled up to my home in Rochester Hills. I liked to believe that I was doing pretty well for myself. I didn't have a mansion or no shit like that, but I had a beautiful four bedroom, three and a half bathroom, three story condominium. I know you probably think it's stupid of me to get this big ass house when I had no kids or anything, but I knew that I wanted to raise my family here.

I rarely brought a bitch to my home, but Renae was slightly different. I did care about her and her feelings. She's the only one that I been fucking with heavy, so I guess I could see why she felt like we were a couple. I parked my car in the garage and we both got out. I damn near forgot I had her riding with me, I was so caught up in my own thoughts.

"I'm going to go ahead and get dinner started. You just relax," she said making sure she walked ahead of me as we headed inside the house.

"Alright," I said and made my way to my room while she got started in the kitchen. One thing I can't take away from shorty, she could cook her ass off. Once I got to my room, I immediately stripped out of my clothes and climbed in the bed. I didn't even realize I had dozed off until I was woken up by the feeling of a warm mouth wrapped around my dick.

"Damn," I moaned in pleasure. Renae got on my motherfucking nerves sometimes, but she knew just how to get me right. A certified soul snatcher. I opened my eyes and watched as her head bobbed up and down on my dick. She looked up at me and took all nine inches in her mouth and gagged which sent me over the edge. Before I knew it, I was shooting my kids all down her throat. That didn't stop her though. She swallowed every ounce of cum until my dick was dry. When she was finished she sat up, wiped her mouth and climbed off the bed.

"The food is ready," she said casually and walked out of the room. I laid there for a moment trying to get my mind right. After about five minutes, I stood up and headed down to the kitchen to see what she had cooked. My mouth watered at the sight of steak, garlic mashed potatoes and broccoli covered with cheese. This was my favorite meal.

"Happy birthday," she said smiling.

"Good looking," I responded as I took my seat at the table. I didn't waste any time digging in to my plate. I savored the first bite because the shit was really as good as it looked.

"Slow down Yasir, it's not going anywhere," she chuckled. I looked up and noticed she had a plate as well.

"Shit good as fuck shorty," I told her with my mouth full. I continued to scarf my food down until I was done. "What's wrong with you?" I asked after noticing that she'd barely touched her food.

"Nothing," she said in a low tone.

"Alright," I said shrugging my shoulders. I knew she was lying, but I wasn't about to force her to talk about it. I excused myself from the table and headed back to my room. I really didn't have any plans. I initially was going to just chill and catch up on some sleep, but now I wanted to get into something. Walking into my room, I grabbed my phone off the nightstand and called up a friend of mine that owned Nikki's night club downtown. I told him to reserve a booth for me and he happily obliged. I might as well go out and have a good time. After making arrangements at the club, I called up my boy Beanie.

"Yo," he answered.

"B, what's the deal?" I responded.

"Ain't shit nigga. Happy Birthday my boy. What you got up?" he asked.

"Good lookin. I wasn't really on shit, but now I'm about to step out. I'mma hit Nicki's tonight. Pull up," I told him.

"Say less my nigga," he said and disconnected the call. I knew Beanie back from way back when. I really didn't have too many niggas that I fucked with because mothafuckas couldn't be trusted, but I knew that whenever I called on Beanie he would be there. In high school, he kept trying to get me to be down with the D-Boyz, a well-known group of dealers in the hood, but I turned it down. I wasn't a pussy or no shit like that, I just wasn't interested in selling drugs. I had other plans for myself and I made that shit happen. I went and got my degree, worked as a mechanical engineer for a while and then got tired of working for people. As a result, I took a leap of faith and branched out with two of my college friends. We ended up starting our own engineering company called 3M and have been successful since we've opened. We have a few major accounts and our team is expanding. It's nothing like getting money the legal way.

Snapping out of my thoughts, I went to my closet to figure out what I was wearing tonight. I never liked to do too much. Usually all black or gray was my go-to. Just because it was my birthday doesn't mean today would be any different. I settled on a black Gucci polo, some black distressed Amiri jeans and my black Gucci sneakers. To accessorize, I added my presidential Rolex that I had iced out as an early birthday gift to myself and my praying hands chain. Just because I didn't sell drugs didn't mean I couldn't look and live like I did. There were other ways to get a bag.

I laid my clothes on the bed and went to take a shower. While I handled my hygiene, my mind kept drifting off to Talayah. I wish I had her number because I would've invited her out tonight, but knowing her mean ass, she would've turned me down anyway. It was something about shorty that I had to have. I could tell that she was used to fucking with lame ass niggas, but I wanted to be the one to change that. I chuckled to myself because I sounded just like a lame ass nigga, but it was the truth. I was gonna break her down, but I wasn't going to hound her.

"Where the fuck you going?" Renae's voice boomed through the bathroom. I sighed as I turned the water off in the shower. Opening the shower door, I found Renae standing there with a mean mug on her face and her arms folded under her titties.

"Out," I said nonchalantly.

"Out where? I thought you said you just wanted to chill in the house. I had something special planned for you," she whined.

"Nah I'm straight. I was gonna stay in, but I don't feel like being stuck in the house on my birthday like a lame ass nigga," I told her, and she sucked her teeth. I ignored her, wrapping the towel around my waist and going to the sink to brush my teeth.

"So, going out with your niggas and entertaining the hoes is better than being laid up and catered to by your girl?" she asked, and I whipped my head in her direction so fast I almost snapped my damn neck.

"You ain't my girl!" I shouted.

"How am I not Yasir? You're the only one I'm fucking with and have been fucking with for months now, and I know I'm the only one you fucking with because ain't no bitches calling your phone and you've been spending all your time with me. I'm here almost all the time Yasir, how are we not together?" she asked, and I put my head down. I guess I had been leading her on, but I thought since neither one of us had talked about making it official she knew what the deal was. Obviously, I thought wrong.

"We never talked about being exclusive. Just because you're the only one that I choose to stick my dick in and spend time with at the moment doesn't mean that you're my girl. I care about you and your feelings, but we never sat down and had that talk. Keep it one hundred like I am. I'd rather keep fucking you than to be out here fucking random bitches and catch something. At least with you I know what I'm getting myself into. You feel me?" I said honestly. I looked over at her and saw the tears in her eyes. Again, I sighed. "I'm not trying to make you cry Renae. I'm just being honest with you," I really hated when females cried, but what could I do? I wasn't trying to hurt her feelings on purpose, I was just trying to be real. Females say they want a nigga to keep it a hundred, but the moment that we do, they crying and shit.

"Bet," was all she said before she exited the room. Moments later I heard the door slam. *Where the fuck is she going? Her car ain't even here*, I thought to myself. The right thing to do would be to go after her and at least offer her a ride home, but I didn't. I continued to get myself together so that I could enjoy my night. It's not my fault she couldn't handle the truth.

Once I was done getting dressed, I sprayed myself with my Gucci Guilty cologne, grabbed my phone and then headed downstairs to grab my keys and hop in the car. I was on my way to the club when my phone rang. The phone was connected to the car via Bluetooth, so I pressed a button to answer.

"Yo."

"Where you at?" my nigga Tone asked. Tone had been my dog since before I went off to college, just like Beanie. I know I said I didn't fuck with niggas like that, and I didn't, but Beanie and Tone were exceptions. They were more like family to me. I trusted the niggas with my life.

"On my way to Nicki's," I told him.

"Bitch, why I gotta hear from Beanie that you tryna step out? I thought yo lame ass would be sleep or some shit by now," he laughed.

"Fuck you. I decided to go ahead and celebrate. Shit, I deserve it," I exclaimed.

"Fasho. Where you at now? Come scoop," he said. Luckily, Tone lived downtown so it was nothing to grab him before heading to the club.

"Bet. Be ready," I said before disconnecting the call.

After scooping Tone from his crib, we made our way to Nicki's which was only a six-minute drive from his house. I parked about a block away and we walked up to the front entrance. It was only ten-thirty and the line was already wrapped around the building. I wasn't tripping on that shit though. I wasn't waiting in line for shit.

Once we made it up to the entrance, I dapped security and made my way in. I heard a few whispers from some hating ass niggas waiting in line, but I ignored it. Niggas were always going to have something to say no matter what, so I just let them talk.

We made our way up the stairs, past the next set of security and finally into the club. Nicki's lounge was basically four clubs in one. Each room had its own bar, dance floor, DJ and booths set up and they all gave off a different vibe. The very first room was decorated in a cream color and was more so for the older folks that enjoyed a good time. When I say older, I mean the mature crowd, thirty-five and up. The next room was more so of a blueish, purpleish design, a little more modern than the first room, where a mixture of age groups flocked to have fun. The other two rooms were for anyone twenty-one and over. My favorite room was in the back, designed in black and gray. In this room, they played a mixture of today's hits, nineties and two-thousands hits and of course today's Detroit music.

"I think every bitch with a fat ass decided to come out tonight. Got damn! Everywhere I look all I see is ass. Its's like I died and went to booty heaven," Tone's ass said excitedly. I chuckled as we continued to walk through the crowd. I found my booth which was right beside the DJ's booth and took a seat. There were already two bottles of Patron and Hennessy in a bucket of ice on the table. Immediately, I grabbed the Hennessy and took it to the head.

"Damn nigga you ain't playin tonight," I heard a familiar voice say. I looked up to see Beanie and his crew and smiled. I stood up, dapped him up and greeted the niggas behind him. "Happy birthday mothafucka," he said over the music.

"Preciate it," I said back. We got comfortable in the booth, talking shit, drinking and having a good time. I observed the crowd and a familiar face caught my eye. *Hell yeah, this is my chance* I thought to myself as I made my way over to the bar where she was standing.

Chapter Seven

Talayah

I know that I shouldn't feel any type of way about a nigga that I didn't know, but for some reason, I was still annoyed. He was so cocky. His entire demeanor told me that he was the shit and he knew it. Then, on top of his cocky ass attitude, he had the nerve to have a girlfriend and still try to get my number. Niggas weren't shit. No matter how fine he was, I was good on him. What did he expect me to do? Fall for him and play the side chick role? Hell no. If that's what he wanted he had the wrong bitch. I had my own problems to be worried about.

Speaking of problems, Antonio's ass had been on his best behavior lately and it was raising all kinds of red flags. I probably should have been happy that he was finally working again and acting like his old self, but every time he did or said something nice to me, I felt like he was on some bullshit. I wanted to leave him, but I didn't know how. I knew he wouldn't leave without a fight, literally. I was just about to pull up to my house when my phone rang. I saw that it was Kree calling me. Immediately, I thought something was wrong at the shop.

"Wassup Kree, everything good?" I asked in a worried tone.

"Yeah everything is straight boss lady. I was just calling to see if you wanted to hang with your girls tonight. Harmony got a free booth at Nicki's tonight and it's free entry before eleven so we're all going," she said.

"Who's we?" I asked.

"Everybody from the shop, Harmony, Kimani, Sarayah and me," she answered.

"Hell yeah, sounds fun. Can I bring Giselle?" I asked.

"Of course, you can," she said, and I agreed to meet them there around ten-thirty. After disconnecting with Kree, I called up

Giselle.

"Wassup bitch," she greeted.

"You wanna step out tonight?" I asked, already knowing she'd be down. Giselle was the turn up queen. She always had been. Don't get it confused though, sis was balanced. She would turn up with you all night and still get up and handle business the next morning. That's why she was my bitch.

"Do people in hell want ice water? Hell yeah. Where we going and who we going with?" she asked.

"Nikki's and my girls from the shop are going. Harmony got a free booth tonight so they're all gonna step out. I told them we would meet there around ten-thirty since it's free before eleven," I told her.

"Yeah I'm down but bitch we ain't gon make it by no ten-thirty. It's damn near nine now," she said.

"You probably right, but still. I'm not waiting in no line and I'm damn sure not paying to get in that bitch," I told her.

"Don't trip. I'mma call Beanie and see if he knows who's working tonight. They'll let us in," she said. Leave it to Beanie to know somebody who works there.

"Alright cool. I'm at the house now, so I'm about to shower and stuff. Meet me here since I'm closer," I told her, and we disconnected. As I walked inside my house, I was feeling good. It had been a long time since I've been out partying with my girls. I usually just liked to stay in the house, read, clean, eat, watch Netflix. Anything that didn't require me being around other people. Giselle always called me lame, but I didn't care.

I walked into my bedroom, throwing my phone, purse, and keys on the bed. I paused for a minute, realizing that Antonio wasn't here. I shrugged it off thinking that he was working late or something. Knowing him, he was probably with his latest side bitch. If I was completely honest with myself, I didn't really care where he was. I welcomed the peace and quiet.

I went into my closet to find something to wear. On a day to day basis, I wore jogging suits and leggings, so I rarely bought any club clothes. My eyes landed on this hot pink jumpsuit that I bought a few months back for this Miami trip Giselle and I were supposed to take, but never did. This was the first piece of clothing I've ever ordered from Fashion Nova, and ever since then, I was hooked. I grabbed a pair of clear heels and set it on the bed, then went to take a shower.

After handling my hygiene, I applied lotion to my body and then proceeded to get dressed. I was about to put on a bra, but remembered that the jumpsuit was cut in the front so that the bottom of my breasts would be showing. Thank God I was in shape. After getting dressed, I stared at myself in the mirror trying to figure out what to do with my hair. I swear, being a girl was so hard. We had so many options. All niggas had to do was get a haircut, put on a shirt and some pants and they were good. I stared in the mirror for a few more minutes before deciding to put my hair in a cute half up half down style with soft curls. I then applied enough make up to my face to make it pop and then glossed my lips. Looking at myself in the mirror, I had to admit, I was a bad bitch. I grabbed my diamond stud earrings, placed them in my ears, put on my favorite heart shaped Pandora ring and diamond cross necklace. I snapped a few selfies on snapchat and uploaded them just as the doorbell rang.

"If you ain't the finest bitch to ever walk! What the fuck!" Giselle shouted, gassing me up. I laughed.

"Bitch you can't talk. Look at you, looking like a whole buffet. Fuck a snack," I said gassing her up in return. She smiled and slightly twerked. If we weren't the finest set of best friends, I didn't know who was.

My girl looked gorgeous. Her caramel skin was flawless. Her face was beat to perfection, but natural at the same time and her sandy brown inches were wand curled. She had on a spaghetti strap neon green mini dress and some clear heels similar to mine.

"Bitch we look like some fucking highlighters," she said, and we laughed simultaneously.

"Fine ass highlighters," I told her and went into the house to grab my purse and keys. Of course, we couldn't leave the house without snapping a few pics and making a few videos for

Instagram and Snapchat. By the time we were ready to leave, it was damn near midnight, but fuck it. We still had a couple of hours to party and have a good time.

We hopped in my car and I pulled off in the direction of the club. Once we got there, I parked about a block away and we walked up to the front entrance.

"Wassup Leon," Giselle said to the bouncer at the front door.

"Wassup G, you looking good as usual," he flirted.

"Yeah I know," she said giggling.

"Go on and have a good time. Your brother just got here not too long ago," he stated, and she nodded her head. We walked past the crowd, up the steps and into the club.

"Which room you wanna go in?" she asked me, and I gave her a knowing look. "Say less sis," she said grabbing my hand and leading me to the room in the back. She knew it was my favorite. As soon as we entered the club, *Thick Bitch* by Icewear Vezzo came booming through the speakers. Vezzo was a well-known Detroit rapper and I fucked with his music heavy. The whole city did.

I'm in love with a thick bitch
I'm in love with a thick bitch
Nigga I'll do whatever for a thick bitch
I'm a boss so my plan is to get rich
I just wanna hit a thick bitch (whaaattt)
I just wanna hit a thick bitch (whaaattt)
I just wanna hit a thick bitch, and if you ain't
got no cash you don't get shit

Giselle and I sang along to the song as we scanned the crowd for Harmony and the rest of the girls. It was hard to tell who was who because the lights were dim and there were so many people in one space.

"BOSS LADY! BOSS LADY!" I heard over the music. I looked in the direction of the voice and saw Kree standing on a booth waving her hand to get my attention. I chuckled. The girl could make her presence known anywhere. Giselle and I greeted the girls and made ourselves comfortable in the booth. I was glad that we were across the room from the DJ booth. That's where the majority of the crowd was, on the dance floor and in the booths closest to it. I hated feeling like I was trapped in the middle of a big crowd. It was calmer where we were, but still lit enough to have a good time.

After about ten or fifteen minutes, Giselle asked me to go with her to the bar to get drinks since the shot girl hadn't made her way back over. We got up from the booth and made our way over to the bar. While Giselle ordered drinks, I casually swayed my hips to the music. I had to admit, I was feeling myself. All of a sudden, City Girls' song Act Up came on and all the females started going crazy, including Giselle and I.

Real ass bitch give a fuck bout a nigga
Big Birkin bag, hold five, six figures
Stripes on my ass so he call this pussy Tigger
Fuckin on a scamming ass, rich ass nigga

Giselle and I immediately started twerking like we were strippers. It's something about City Girls and Cardi B that could bring out the inner hood rat in a female. We twerked at the bar the entire time the song played, laughing and having fun. A couple of weak ass niggas tried to get behind us, but we weren't having that. As the song went off, I couldn't help but to feel a pair of eyes on me. I scanned the crowd thinking Harmony or one of the girls was trying to get my attention, but when I looked over at them, they were throwing back shots, twerking and standing on the booth, getting lit. I continued to scan the room and almost came on myself when my eyes locked with Yasir's fine ass. He licked his lips and I watched as he stepped out of the booth closest to the DJ and made his way towards me.

He looked so fucking good in his all black Gucci fit. I just saw him earlier, but it felt like I was seeing him for the very first time. That smooth chocolatey skin and that beard did something to me.

"Happy birthday," I said as soon as he approached me.

"It is now," he said licking his lips seductively. I blushed and turned my head, trying to hide my face from him. "You look beautiful," he complimented.

"Thanks, you don't look so bad yourself," He grabbed my waist and brought me closer to him.

"You and your girl should come chill in our booth," he said in my ear. His breath smelled like mint, and the feeling of it in my ear sent a chill down my spine. Why was I reacting this way?

"I'm with my girls right now. We got our own booth," I told him. Yasir looked at me like he wanted to say something, but instead he nodded his head.

"That's cool. If you change your mind, you know where I'll be. I really wanna spend my birthday with you though."

"Shouldn't you be spending your birthday with your girl?" I asked. I know I was being petty, but I just couldn't help it. It was the only way that I could fight the way he made me feel. I looked up at him and he had an irritated expression on his face. He even let his grip around my waist go.

"That's not my girl. I don't know how many times I gotta say that shit to you. Enjoy your night Talayah. Remember what I said," he said before kissing me on the cheek and walking off. I stood there for what felt like minutes before Giselle nudged me.

"You better stop playing with that fine ass nigga," she said laughing and moving her head to the beat. I could tell she was drunk.

"Ain't nobody playing with him. I just think it's funny how he keeps pursuing me knowing that he has somebody. I ain't nobody's side bitch," I told her, and she giggled.

"Yeah okay best friend. Here," she said handing me a drink. "Drink this and loosen up," I took the drink from her hand and sipped. I realized that it was a drink they had called Wet Pussy, which I loved. I gulped the rest down and headed back to the booth with the girls.

"Where the hell were you?" Harmony asked once I made my way back to the booth.

"On the dance floor," I said casually. We continued to enjoy our night, but I couldn't help but to steal glances at Yasir. Every inch of me wanted to go over there and turn up with him.

Chapter Eight

Yasir

After running into Talayah at the club, I couldn't keep my eyes off of her. She looked good as fuck in that jumpsuit, and she knew it. As bad as I wanted her to come up here with me, I couldn't force her to.

"Aye nigga, why the fuck you over here looking like a sad ass puppy?" Beanie said slurring. This nigga was drunk as fuck. I laughed, watching him struggle to keep his balance. He could never hold his liquor, and when he was drunk, he acted a fucking fool.

"Nigga you acting like it's your birthday and shit. Drunk ass," I said laughing.

"Every day is my birthday," he said smiling. I couldn't do nothing but shake my head at him. "Is that my sister?" he asked, and I looked in the direction that he was pointing in. My eyes landed on Talayah and the girl she was with. I didn't even realize that was Giselle or that the two of them were friends. I never knew what Giselle looked like for real because I was never around her growing up. I wish I would have been though, I would have bumped into Talayah sooner.

I watched as Beanie made his way through the crowd, stumbling every couple of steps towards Giselle and Talayah. They hugged, exchanged a few words and then Beanie pointed his finger up to our booth. I saw a slight smile on Talayah's face but it quickly disappeared. She was trying her hardest to put up a front and I had to admit that shit was cute. It let me know that she wasn't like these other females out here. Had she been any other female I probably would've fucked her by now. I couldn't keep my eyes off of her as she followed her girl up to our booth. Every nigga she passed stopped and did a double take. I just knew she was going to be mine, someway, somehow. I just had to get her away from the bitch ass nigga she thought she loved.

"I see you made your way to me anyways," I said smirking.

"Whatever nigga," she said sitting next to me.

"You look good as fuck," I said in her ear.

"Thank you Yasir," she replied. The way she said my name made my dick hard. I subtly adjusted myself.

"You want something to drink?" I asked her. She nodded her head. "What you want?" I asked. She looked at the bottles on the table and shook her head no, standing up and flagging down the bottle girl.

"Can I have a bottle of Rose?" she asked.

"Me too," Giselle said, and the bottle girl nodded, turning to walk away. All of a sudden, Back That Ass Up by Juvenile came on and the entire club started going crazy, including Giselle and Talayah.

"Bitch this is my shit!" Talayah said swinging her hair from side to side. As soon as the beat dropped, Talayah started shaking her ass and I promise it took everything in me not to snatch her little ass up, take her in the bathroom and fuck the shit out of her. Who knew somebody so little could be so fucking bad. The way her ass jiggled in that jumpsuit had my dick harder than it had ever been. She flipped her hair to the right, looked back at me and smiled. I signaled for her to come over to me and she twerked backwards until she was on my lap.

"Got damn," I said under my breath. Talayah and I were in the zone until she was yanked off of my lap.

"Oh hell naw!" Giselle yelled swinging on whoever had yanked Talayah off of me. I couldn't see Talayah but I could tell Giselle was giving it to whoever it was. I couldn't really tell because the club was so dark, and by this time Giselle had ole girl on the floor. Talayah was able to get off the floor and started kicking the shit out the bitch. Beanie went over and pulled Giselle off of the girl.

"Dumb ass hoe! Keep your mothafucking hands to yourself!" Giselle screamed. The girl was in a fetal position for a few moments before she finally stood up. When I realized who it was, it took everything in me to contain my laugh.

"Renae what the fuck is your problem?" I yelled.

"You left me to come to the club and fuck around with these thot ass bitches?!" she yelled. Her hair was all over the place and her lip was busted. She was even holding her side where Talayah had kicked her repeatedly. Before I could say anything else Talayah cocked back and hit her with a mean left sending her back down to the ground.

"Bitch watch yo poor ass mouth!" she screamed.

"Damn Lay Lay," Beanie said laughing, causing the whole crew to laugh as well. Unable to control it any longer, I bust out laughing right along with them. The bouncers came our way and escorted Renae out kicking and screaming. I looked around and noticed that the music had stopped, and all eyes were on us. Once Renae left, the music started again, and people went back to drinking and laughing like nothing ever happened. I reached for Talayah, but she snatched her arm away from me.

"I'm ready to go G," she spoke to Giselle, completely ignoring me.

"Alright, let me see if the girls are still here and we can go," Giselle told her and Talayah nodded her head.

"Talayah," I called, and she walked away. "Talayah!" I repeated, but she kept walking. Just when she was starting to get comfortable, this bitch Renae had to fuck it up, and I didn't even get a chance to get her number. I knew she had mine, but she hadn't used it, and I knew she really wasn't going to use it after tonight.

Chapter Nine

Talayah

It had been two weeks since that incident at Niki's and I hadn't heard from or seen Yasir, and I was okay with that. It was no way I was fucking around with a nigga and fighting his hoes every time we were in public together. As much as I was feeling him, I couldn't allow myself to go down that road. Plus, I still had a whole nigga at home.

Speaking of, Antonio's ass has been MIA for the past week. I texted and called him a few times, but he completely ignored me. I knew that act wouldn't last long. At this point, I knew he was laid up with the next bitch and as much as I tried to convince myself that I didn't give it fuck, it still hurt my feelings. What else could he possibly be doing for him to stay away for a fucking week? The only reason why I wasn't pressed is because whatever he was doing in the dark was going to come to the light. My Mama always told me that and I lived by it.

I had been working my ass off at the shop lately just to keep busy. I didn't really have shit else to do, so I might as well run up a check. When I walked into the house, the smell of weed filled my nostrils and I rolled my eyes. The one day I wanted to come home and just relax and have some time to myself, his ass decided to come back. I didn't feel like dealing with any of his bullshit. Walking into my room, I found Antonio sprawled out, smoking a blunt in his underwear. I ignored him and started to strip out of my clothes to take a shower.

"You don't see me laying here?" he asked. I continued to ignore him and made my way to the shower. Just as I was about to close the door, he grabbed my arm to spin me around. I snatched away from him. "You gon act like you don't see me?" he asked raising his voice.

"Antonio don't say shit to me. I haven't seen or heard from yo ass in a week and you want to come back acting like everything is all good? Fuck out of here," I said to him. I ran the water for a shower and waited for it to heat up.

"Man, I've been working like a mothafucka. Literally back to back shifts. I just grabbed a room for the week until I had a few days off," he said, and I frowned.

"That's the weakest excuse I've ever heard. You really think I'm dumb as fuck, huh? Who the fuck gets a room because they're working back to back shifts. And if that's the case why didn't you come back to grab no clothes, a toothbrush or anything? I know you ain't making that much money that you can just go and buy new shit," I stated. He just stood there staring at me with a blank expression on his face.

"Exactly," I told him. "Get out of my face Antonio," he sucked his teeth, but didn't say anything, just walked out of the bathroom. I proceeded to get in the shower and wash my ass. It seems like every nigga that I came in contact with was full of shit. The nigga that I had was cheating on me with some random bitch or bitches and the nigga that I wanted had a whole girlfriend. He said he didn't, but I wasn't dumb. No bitch was going to be in the club fighting for no reason. If she was doing all that it's because he was giving her a reason to.

I finished up my shower, lotioned my body and put on an oversized t-shirt and panties. I climbed into the bed next to Antonio. I felt so stupid for letting this nigga cheat on me and then come back like nothing happened. He'd been doing it for so long, I guess I was kind of immune to it. All I did was cuss him out and then act like nothing ever happened.

At first, it was very subtle, but now, he might as well have just brought the bitches here. He pulled me closer, and I wanted to push him away from me, but I didn't. I wasn't in love with this man anymore, but I still had love for him. Even though I really didn't want him, I didn't want to leave him. I felt like I had put too much time and effort to just let whatever bitch have him. We had been through so much, not even Giselle knew everything.

"Bae, I know you feel some type of way, but I promise you, I been grinding non-stop. I'm trying to make it so I can give you all that shit we've talked about. The house, the cars, the ring, everything. I love you Talayah. I always have and I always will," he said kissing me on the forehead. I didn't respond, I just laid my head on his chest and silently cried.

Antonio

I felt fucked up for lying to Talayah's face like that, but I had to think of something. I really had been working my ass off, but I wasn't laying my head at a hotel. I'd been chilling and fucking the shit out of LaCorsha. The only reason I came back to Talayah's house is because LaCorsha was starting to get on my fucking nerves. I stayed at her house for a few days and she acted like we were a fucking married couple or some shit. She kept asking me to take out the trash and all types of shit. The bitch even had the nerve to ask me about helping out with some of her bills. I took that as my queue to get the fuck on and go back to my bitch. Co had gotten way too comfortable with me being there.

I looked down and realized Talayah had gone to sleep and hadn't cooked or done shit. Instantly, I became irritated. As much as Co got on my nerves, she was definitely taking care of a nigga the way a woman should. She cooked damn near every day for a nigga, cleaned, rubbed my feet, and of course she was giving that pussy up whenever I wanted it. She was really catering to a nigga, but I just couldn't commit to her. As fucked up as I treated Talayah sometimes, she had my heart, and I'll be damned if I let her ass go. She would die first, and that's on my life.

I grabbed my phone off of the night stand and realized that I had four missed calls from none other than LaCorsha. I started not to call her back until I received a text message from her saying it was urgent.

"Antonio," she said into the phone. She sounded sad as fuck and I immediately thought somebody died.

"What's up?" I asked.

"I need you to come over right now. We need to talk," she said.

"About what?"

"Please just come Antonio. I wouldn't be calling you like that if it wasn't serious," she said sniffling. It seemed like she was crying.

"Alright man, I'll be there in a minute. Stop with that crying shit," I told her. I looked down at Talayah again, and she was still fast asleep. I gently pulled her off my chest and hopped off of the bed. I ordered an Uber and put my clothes on. I sat on the bed waiting for the Uber, wondering what the hell LaCorsha could have possibly wanted. I was just over her house last night. What could have happened between now and then?

Once my Uber was outside, I ran out and hopped in. It took about ten to fifteen minutes to make it to her house. LaCorsha lived in Southfield in a nice little two-story traditional home with an attached two car garage. One thing about me, a nigga had taste. I didn't fuck with just any bitch with a fat ass. They had to have something going for themselves. I mean, she was still dancing, but shit it paid her bills and kept her living the lifestyle that she'd grown accustomed to. I couldn't hate on her hustle. Once I made it to her front door, I knocked and rang the doorbell. Almost immediately, she opened the door with tears coming down her cheeks.

"What's wrong?" I asked.

"Come in," she said opening the door wider for me to walk through. She led me to her living room, and I took a seat on the sectional that sat in the middle of the room.

"What's up Co?" I asked again getting impatient. I was starting to feel like she called me over here for no reason. Wasting my damn time. She looked at me and then disappeared into the bathroom. A few moments later she came out of the bathroom with something behind her back.

"Please don't get mad," she said nervously.

"Man spit it out!" I yelled causing her to jump a little bit. She handed me a white stick and I looked at it confused until I saw the word *Pregnant* on the screen. I swear it felt like the entire world stopped spinning.

"Are you sure?" I asked and she gave me a blank stare.

"I made an emergency doctor's appointment for tomorrow so I'm going to make sure. I'm scared as fuck Antonio. I don't know what to do with no baby," she said starting to cry again.

"Are you sure it's mine?" I asked and she frowned.

"I wouldn't have called you if I didn't think it was yours Antonio. You the only one I've been fucking, and you know it," she said with a slight attitude.

"Man, fuck!" I yelled throwing the test on the floor. What the fuck am I going to do with a kid? A kid that's not Talayah's at that. Fuck, Talayah. She was going to fucking kill me. I just knew it.

• •

Two Weeks Later

Once again, I fucked up, staying at LaCorsha's house for longer than I should have. For the past two weeks her ass has been stuck to me like glue. She was two minutes pregnant acting like she was set to give birth at any minute. To make matters even worse, Talayah had been blowing my phone up and I was ignoring her. I wasn't ready to go back home to all that bitching and nagging that I knew was bound to happen. The shit was probably my fault, but damn. I had my reasons for doing what I did. Maybe I just wasn't a one-woman man. Especially when that woman acted more like my Mama than my girl.

"Tony!" I heard LaCorsha yell from downstairs. I rubbed my hand down my face, already irritated by whatever the fuck she was about to say.

"What?" I responded.

"Come here," she said, and I groaned. Begrudgingly, I got up from the bed and went downstairs to see what her irritating ass wanted. I found her in the kitchen sitting on the floor with her knees to her chest and her back against the wall.

"What the hell wrong with you?" I asked frowning.

"Something's not right," she said looking at me.

"What you mean? What's wrong?" I asked looking at her in

confusion.

"My stomach is killing me. I can't keep anything down. Food, juice, pop, water, nothing," she said and started crying. I sucked my teeth. I hated when females cried. It irritated me but it was also a soft spot.

"Man, relax. Do you want me to take you to urgent care or the hospital?" I asked.

"No, can you just carry me to the room?" she asked. I looked at her and I could have sworn I saw a smirk.

"Man, ain't shit wrong with you. Fuck out of here," I said walking away from her.

"Antonio! Get back here! I'm your child's mother! I need you!" she begged and I ignored her. She kept pulling little dumb ass stunts like something was really wrong with her and I fell for it every time. I started to go back up the steps to the room, but then turned around and went back into the kitchen.

"Look, you a grown ass woman Co and you doing the most. You know I'm gonna be around for you and my seed but stop trying to force us to be something that we ain't right now. Trying to force me to cater to you and do all that boyfriend shit ain't gon make me want you so chill out. I'm about to get my shit and head back home. I think we both need some space from each other. Just call me when it's time for your first appointment and I'll be there," I said and left her sitting on the kitchen floor.

I really didn't feel like going to Talayah's. She wasn't going to do anything but stress me out more than I already was. My only other choice was to head to my favorite place, the bar.

Talayah

I was really over this shit with Antonio. First, he stays gone for a week and now it's been almost three weeks and I haven't heard shit from his ass. My patience was running so thin with this nigga. I feel stupid for falling for that same ole line that he ran on me every time he was out on his bullshit.

I was just about to call him when my front door flew open. I looked up and sure enough, it was Antonio looking a fucking mess. It looked like he hadn't seen a barbershop in a month, and he reeked of liquor. I could smell him from the other side of the room. I instantly knew that some shit was about to go down.

He staggered his drunk ass in the house, barely able to stand. Just as he was closing the door, I noticed a nice black truck in the driveway. I couldn't quite make out the make and model, but I knew it wasn't mine.

"Whose car is that?" I asked. He smirked at me before responding.

"That's my shit," he said cockily. I frowned my face.

"Yours? Since when did you buy a car?" I asked in confusion. This nigga hasn't contributed to shit in this house since he started working again and he goes and buys himself a car?

"Since I did. Why are you counting my pockets?" he asked slurring his words.

"You ain't shit! I swear! You so fucking triflin'! You laid yo ass up in this house for months while I held everything down. You finally get a job and start making some money and you disappear on me, pop up whenever you want to and show up with a car? Are you serious? You don't think you should contribute to the place you've laid your head at?" I asked, neck rolling, arms folded and everything.

"Bitch watch yo mothafuckin mouth. That's yo fuckin problem. You talk too much. Just shut the fuck up. This is why I stay gone all the fucking time because you always bitching!" he yelled stumbling over towards me. As soon as he got within arm's reach, I drew my arm back and slapped the taste out of his mouth. He glared at me with menacing eyes and I gave him a look back that dared him to try me.

"Nigga I wish you would!" I yelled. "I'm bitching because of the shit that you do! You ever stop to think about that!? You act right for two seconds and think you doing something. You've been gone off and on for damn near a month Antonio and you got the nerve to come in this bitch talkin shit?! I should beat yo mothafuckin ass!" I yelled punching him in the chest over and over. I was so fucking tired of him. I was tired of letting everything roll off of my shoulders like I wasn't hurt. He had been doing me so dirty for so long and I kept ignoring it? For what? Why was I stuck in this relationship with a man who clearly didn't give a fuck about me? He only cared about what I could provide to him and now that he was making his own money again, it was fuck me.

I looked up at Antonio and I saw a look in his eyes that I had never seen before. He's hit me a few times, but this look was something different. I had to admit for the first time in my life, I was scared as fuck of what he might do, but I would never show it. Antonio looked at me and grinned. It was an evil grin, and before I could blink, he hit me right in my nose. I instantly dropped down to the ground. This nigga had hit me like I was some random person on the street.

"Keep your mothafuckin hands off me! I done told you about that smart-ass mouth! Maybe if you were acting more like the woman a nigga needed, I wouldn't have to be out for weeks at a time looking for what I don't fucking have in another bitch. I wanted a family, I wanted to marry you. I was going to give you everything you fucking wanted. Instead of nagging and giving up on me you should've stayed down. I was fucked up, but I wasn't going to be fucked up forever. Yeah, I could've done a lot of things better but you ain't have my back. Having my support system was half the battle! Man, fuck you!" he yelled punching me over and over and then kicking me in my stomach. He continued to pound on me and tell me how much he hated me until he was out of breath. I couldn't do anything but ball up in a fetal position and try to shield my face from his kicks and blows.

"Antonio please stop! It's me!" I managed to get out, but my pleas fell on deaf ears. It was like he had blacked out and didn't even realize that he was pounding on me like I was just a sack of potatoes.

Finally, after what felt like hours of being beaten on, he stopped. I wanted to move, but my body felt like I had been run over by a car. I heard him go to the back, but I still couldn't move. I laid there crying, hoping that this was just a nightmare and that someone would come and save me, but nothing happened.

I laid there and thought of the times when my Mama and Daddy would argue and he would beat her ass. Even though I loved both of my parents to death, I couldn't act like the past didn't exist. My Daddy and Antonio favored each other in so many ways, it's no wonder they got along so well. Daddy used to stay gone and at the time, I thought he was just working hard. Come to find out he was out acting like he didn't have a wife and kid at home. Whenever my Mom would confront him about it, he beat her ass. After a while, my Mom just stopped asking. When I was in high school, I asked her why she didn't leave, and she said that it was because she loved him and there was no since in doing all that fighting and hollering if she was going to stay. I resented her for so long, but I acted like everything was okay. Nobody but Giselle knew about the feelings that I harbored for my parents. Not even Antonio, even though I knew our stories were very similar. It was just too embarrassing to talk about and if Antonio knew about it, he would certainly find a way to use it for his benefit.

Antonio's foot stomping on my arm quickly brought me out of my thoughts. I managed to open my eyes and saw him with some bags in his hands. He set the bags down, grabbed his keys, taking a single key off of the ring and throwing it at me.

"Wake the fuck up! I just wanted to tell yo ass that you

ain't gotta worry about me no more. I won't be back," he said and walked out the door. I laid there crying my eyes out wishing I would wake up from this nightmare. I felt so stupid, but I knew that I was no better than all the bitches me and Giselle used to sit and talk shit about.

After he left, I looked around searching for my phone. Luckily, it wasn't too far away on the floor. I managed to crawl to my phone and call Giselle.

"Fuck," I mumbled to myself after she didn't answer. I laid there crying thinking of who I could call. I could only think of one other person to call, and as much as I didn't want to, I couldn't think of anyone else that would come through for me.

Yasir

It's been damn near a month since my birthday and the incident between Talayah, Giselle, and Renae. I'd been ignoring Renae's ass like the plague. I really didn't have shit to say to her after the way she showed her ass. At the end of the day, I was still a single man, so what I did and who I did it with was none of her concern.

Not only have I been off these other bitches, my mind was fixed on Talayah's little ass. As much as I hated to say it, she had me feeling some type of way. I wanted to reach out to her, but I didn't have her number. I even went up to her shop a couple of times but she wasn't there. Either that or she was telling her receptionist to say she wasn't there. One way or another, I was going to get to her.

Knock! Knock! The sound of knocking on my office door broke me from my thoughts of Talayah.

"Come in," I said. A few moments later Renae walked through the door. Out of reflex I sighed, and she frowned.

"My presence is irritating to you now?" she said with an attitude. I was here trying to work, I really didn't want to deal with this right now.

"What's up Renae? Why are you here?" I asked.

"Well since you've been ignoring me I wanted to come and talk to you," she said taking a seat in the chair across from the desk.

"I really don't have anything to say to you. As a matter of fact, I really don't want to fuck with you anymore. I think that I may have lead you on and made you think that we were something we weren't. That shit you pulled at the club was uncalled for. I ain't feeling that at all," I said honestly. She looked at me with tears in her eyes, but I wasn't fazed by it. I always kept it a

60

hundred with everybody I came in contact with whether they like it or not.

"Is it because of that bitch at the club?" she asked.

"First of all, watch your mouth. Second of all, that's none of your business if it is. I just don't like the way you move. Don't get me wrong, you're a good girl, just not the girl that I want or need," I said calmly. I thought she was about to cuss me out and trash my office, but instead, she nodded her head and turned to walk out of the door. I rubbed my hand over my face. These females were going to be the death of me.

"Mr. White?" I heard my assistant Camille say. I looked up to see what it is she needed.

"What can I do for you Camille?" I asked.

"I have Mr. Antonio James from the Southfield plant here, he'd like to speak with you," she told me, and I nodded my head. I didn't know who the hell Antonio James was, but I was always willing to sit down and speak to any of my employees. I told Camille to send him in and a few minutes later, a man who looked like he'd been working his ass off strolled in my office. He was dressed down in some black jeans, work boots and a hoodie, but from the look on his face I could tell that he was tired. I stood up to shake his hand. His hand shake was firm, which was a good sign.

"Nice to meet you Mr. James," I stated.

"Likewise," he said.

"What can I do for you?" I asked motioning for him to take a seat in the chair that Renae was sitting in. He sat down and folded his hands on top of my desk, and looked me right in the eyes.

"Mr. White, I've only been here for a few months, but in this short time, I've noticed that there are some qualities that your management team is lacking," he stated. I looked at him with a blank expression. My interest had been peaked, but I would never let him know that. Nobody had ever come to me about my management team before, so I was interested in what he had to say.

"Qualities like what?" I asked him. He went on to tell me that some of the people that I've chosen to be in leadership were taking their position to the head. My supervisors were talking down to my line workers and treating them like they were less than. I didn't like that shit at all. I wanted each and every one of my employees to feel valued. No one was better than the next.

"I'm coming to you because I enjoy the work that I do, and the majority of the people that I work with. I don't plan on leaving any time soon, but in order to keep your front-line employees, they have to feel like they matter. Nobody else is going to come to you and express how they feel out of fear that they'll lose their job, but somebody had to. That someone might as well be me," he said confidently. I liked this guy. He seemed to be very determined and didn't take any shit. The fact that he had the balls to come and talk to me like a man said a lot.

"Tell me something," I started. "Are you coming to me saying all of this because you want to be a supervisor?" I asked. I had to know what his end game was, even though I already had a feeling.

"I'm not going to lie to you, I would love to be a supervisor. That's always been my plan. I don't plan to stay on the line forever. I have a degree in mechanical engineering that can go way beyond working on the line, but I know that I have to start from the bottom to get to the top," he said, and I nodded my head.

"Good answer," I said standing up, and he followed suit. I extended my arm to shake his hand. "We'll most definitely be in touch," I told him, and he nodded his head then left out of my office. I needed people like him on my team. If my employees weren't going to stand for what's right, I'd have a bunch of yes men working for me and I didn't want that. Just as I was about to leave out of my office, my phone vibrated. I looked at the number and didn't recognize it, which caused a frown on my face, but I answered anyway.

"Yo."

"Yasir?" a sweet and innocent voice said on the other line. I've only run into her a few times but I knew her voice anywhere.

"Talayah?"

"Yes," she said sniffling.

"Are you crying?" I asked. It was silent for a while and then I heard her break down. "Talayah talk to me. What's wrong?" I was genuinely concerned about her. Especially because this was her first time calling me and because she was crying. I hated for women to cry. Well, most women, some women I didn't give a fuck about. She cried for a few more moments before she calmed down and then she spoke.

"Yasir, I need you. Are you busy?" she asked. It sounded like she was in pain or sick.

"Naw, I was actually just leaving work. Where are you? Are you ok?" I asked.

"No. I'll send you my location," she said, and I agreed. We disconnected and a few seconds later she had sent me her location. I didn't know what was wrong with her, but if it had anything to do with her bitch ass boyfriend, I wouldn't hesitate to handle him for her.

Antonio

I walked out of Mr. White's office feeling super confident. I planned on eliminating my competition at work and that conversation was just the beginning. Surprisingly, shit had been going good in my life since that incident between Talayah and I. I reached out to her numerous times trying to apologize, but she wasn't trying to hear that shit. I should have known that though. Talayah didn't play that shit. Granted, it wasn't the first time I fucked up and put my hands on her, but never to that magnitude. I knew for a fact that she was done with me and I wasn't even going to put my energy into getting her back. I may have made some dumb ass decisions, but I was smart. If I tried to get back with Talayah right now, knowing LaCorsha was pregnant, that would only create more problems that I didn't want.

Speaking of LaCorsha, I've practically been shacking up with her since I walked out on Talayah. I know I said I wanted to get away from her ass, but I was basically drawn to her, like a moth to a fucking flame. She hadn't been that bad either. I threatened to beat her ass one day and ever since then she's been on the straight and narrow. It seemed like that's what I had to resort to in order to get these females in check. They start running off at the mouth and thinking they run shit until I show them who's really running shit.

I hopped into my car and headed towards LaCorsha's house. I was feeling good and I wanted to celebrate. Hopefully she was up to it. Her ass had been throwing up and all types of shit lately.

It took me about fifteen minutes to pull up to the house. I got out and went to the front door, unlocking it with the key she gave me. As soon as I waked in the house the smell of a home cooked meal filled my nostrils. A smile spread on my face. LaCorsha was working over-time to make sure a nigga was satisfied, and I wasn't complaining. I wished it would have been this easy to get Talayah's ass in line, but I guess it is what it is. I would try and get back with her once the baby was born, and that's if I even still wanted her.

Walking in the kitchen I saw LaCorsha standing over the stove in an oversized t-shirt and nothing else. That shit instantly made my dick hard. I walked over to her, wrapped my arms around her waist and kissed her neck.

"How was work babe?" she asked.

"Good as hell. I had that talk with my boss today and I'm pretty sure he took what I said into consideration. He looked like he was shocked that I was actually speaking up and I know he respected it," I told her. She looked back at me and smiled then pecked my lips.

"That's good baby, I'm proud of you," she told me. I smiled at her but inwardly found myself comparing her to Talayah. Why couldn't Talayah be supportive like this? Why couldn't I come home and she's cooking? The little things mattered. She tried to act like it was all me, but it wasn't. It takes two to make a relationship work or destroy it.

"What are you thinking about?" LaCorsha asked bringing me out of my thoughts.

"Nothing," I said kissing her cheek and rubbing on her belly. It still fucked me up that I was having a baby with somebody that wasn't Talayah. I thought I was going to spend the rest of my life with her. I planned on proposing and everything. I know y'all are probably so tired of me talking about her, but I couldn't help it. As much as I tried to act hard, I did miss her sometimes.

I shook my head attempting to clear thoughts of Talayah out of my head. LaCorsha knew when some shit was up with me and I didn't feel like arguing with her ass about my ex. All she would do is talk shit about how she's pregnant and I'm disrespecting her. I let her continue to cook in the kitchen while I went to the living room to relax. I needed to find a way to be happy with what I have and not trip on what I lost, especially since I'm the one that walked out. But like I said before, Talayah was always going to be mine and she would die before I let her move on and be happy without me. Fuck that.

Chapter Fourteen

Talayah

KNOCK! KNOCK! KNOCK!

I knew it could only be Yasir banging on my door like that. I tried to get up, but it hurt to move. Thankfully my phone was still in my hand so I called him.

"Open the door. I'm outside," he said.

"I know. I can't move," I said whimpering. "I think...the door is unlocked," I said and a few seconds later the door opened. I saw Yasir walking towards me out of the corner of my eye.

"What the fuck happened?" he asked in an angry yet concerned tone. I couldn't answer him; all I could do was cry. He rubbed my head trying to comfort me. "I gotta get you to the hospital," he said.

"No!" I shouted. "I'm...fine," I said struggling to sit up.

"Man, you ain't fine. I'm taking you to the hospital Lay, it ain't shit you can say or do to stop me," he said, and I let him pick me up and carry me to his car. It hurt like hell to even be touched, but I was grateful that he came through for me. The ride to the hospital as well as the entire visit was silent. Yasir didn't ask me any questions and I didn't volunteer any information. I knew the questions were coming though, but I would deal with them when they came.

• •

It had been a few days since Antonio walked out and I was fucked up. I hadn't been to the shop in days because I didn't want anyone to see me with my arm in a sling and my body and face bruised. All I could do was lay in the bed, cry and sleep. I wasn't eating, I wasn't showering, I wasn't doing anything that a normal person would do. Honestly, I was scaring myself. I'd never felt this low and I felt like I needed somebody. I didn't want to call anyone close to me because I felt like they wouldn't understand.

I hadn't talked to Yasir since he dropped me back off at home, but I felt like I needed him right now. He had been respecting my space and had only reached out via text to make sure I was ok and to see if I needed anything. Reluctantly, I called him over again today to keep me company, but now that I think about it, I probably should've stayed to myself. He didn't even know me like that to be dealing with my emotional and mental breakdowns. He'd already done enough just showing up and taking me to the hospital.

The sound of somebody banging on my front door broke me away from my thoughts. I got out of the bed and went to open the front door. Laying eyes on Yasir, I quickly became conscious of my appearance. I know I looked a mess. I hadn't touched my hair in days, and I hadn't really showered either. I know, it's nasty. Don't judge me.

"What's wrong?" he asked with a worried expression on his face. I broke away from his stare and looked down at the floor. I knew the time had come for me to explain what was going on. How do I find the words to say to this man? How do I express how I allowed somebody to use and mistreat me for so long?

"Talayah, what's wrong?" he asked again, using his thumb and index finger to lift my chin, causing me to look him in the eyes. I didn't say anything to him as the tears filled my eyes.

"Man, come here," he said hugging me. The moment that our bodies connected, I broke down crying. It felt like the tears I was releasing came from a different place deep down in my soul. I cried for all the times I allowed myself to be talked down to, beat on, lied to, and cheated on. I cried for allowing myself to become all the girls I talked shit about but became just like. I cried for allowing myself to lower my standards and believe that being treated the way that Antonio did me was ok.

After what felt like hours of me crying into his chest, I finally calmed down and led Yasir to the couch. We sat next to each other for a few minutes in silence before he spoke.

"Talk to me," he said, and I took a deep breath.

"I've just been feeling like I failed. I grew up to be the very thing that I never wanted to be," I told him.

"What do you mean? You're a strong, smart, gorgeous black queen. You have your own crib, car, house and business. How have you failed?" he asked and I shook my head.

"That's just what's on the outside. Yeah, on the surface my life is lit, but nobody really knows what goes on behind closed doors," I told him.

"Well, what does go on behind closed doors? I'd like to understand why you feel the way that you do."

"Growing up, I watched girls fall in love with these lame ass niggas and get done so wrong. Me and Giselle used to talk heavy shit about 'em. We vowed that we would never let a nigga think we loved them so much that being lied to, cheated on, and abused was okay. We said we would never be that stupid. I even watched my own Daddy cheat and beat on my Mom and I hated her for staying with him," I said holding back more tears. "Then, I met Antonio and I fell in love and somewhere down the line I started allowing him to do whatever the fuck he wanted," I looked over at him and saw his jaw was clenched tightly. "Never mind," I quickly said.

"No, I want you to be able to talk to me about any and everything. I'm not here to judge you. I'm here to listen to you. I think that's the reason you called me. You need somebody that'll listen to you and be there for you. I know we don't know each other that well but I want to be that, if you'll let me," he said, and I broke down again. I didn't want Yasir to see me so vulnerable but it was hard not to. His entire vibe felt safe and comforting, something that I've never experienced from a man before. Especially a man who barely knew me.

Once I was able to get myself together, I told him all about my relationship with Antonio and even went into detail about my parents. The entire time that I spoke he never took his eyes off of me. He never gave me a judgmental look and he didn't interrupt when I spoke. He literally sat there and listened to me and it felt good to get everything off of my chest that I was holding back.

"I just feel so stupid," I said after taking a deep breath.

"Don't feel stupid. You can't beat yourself up about it. All you can do is learn from it. Plus, it's not completely your fault. Kids are very impressionable, so even though deep down you knew what your Dad was doing was wrong, you were programmed to believe that's the way it is because you didn't know any better. You weren't shown anything different to go off of. It happens to the best of us. Even me. I didn't have my Dad around at all. I don't even know who that nigga is. My Mama raised me all by herself so I had to be the man of the house. Granted, I never got into that street shit or nothing like that, but I know plenty of niggas who have. My nigga Beanie is a prime example," he said, and I whipped my head in his direction.

"Oh yeah! I forgot Beanie was with you that night at the club. That's crazy that you know him and I never ran into you before. You know that's Giselle's brother, right?" I told him and he nodded.

"That shit is crazy as hell. Me and Beanie been down since before high school. That's my dawg fasho. I think we never crossed paths because I was never really around. My Mama made sure my head was in them books and not in the streets," he said chuckling and I slightly smiled.

"That's good. I can tell she raised a good man," I told him.

"I like to think so. But back to you. I don't want you to think that what that nigga did to you is okay. You deserve better than that Talayah, straight up. You deserve to be treated like the Queen that you are. I see that shit even if you don't see it for your damn self," he said, and I nervously looked down at my hands in my lap. He pulled my body into his chest and kissed the top of my head. "I don't want you to waste another tear on that nigga, you hear me? I'm in your life now and I ain't going nowhere unless you want me to. Shit, if you need me to handle that nigga, I will," he said in a stern tone. I lifted my body so that I could look at him.

"Handle him like how?" I asked, even though I already knew the answer. He gave me a knowing look and I shook my head. "You ain't gotta do all of that Yasir," I told hm.

"Just say the word and I got you. I mean that shit on

everything," he said, and I nodded. I was just about to lay my head on his chest again, but then I thought about something.

"Don't you have a whole girlfriend?" I asked and he shook his head.

"She ain't my girl and she ain't shit to me no more. I've been cool on her since my birthday," he said, and I believed him.

"Yeah alright. Let that bitch come at me sideways and I'mma beat her ass again," I said, and he chuckled.

"Relax. Yo little ass don't need to be fighting nobody but the shower right now," he said, and I playfully punched him in the arm. He held up his hands in mock surrender. "I'm just saying, what kind of friend would I be if I let you be in my presence smelling like bounce that ass?" he said and bust out laughing. I rolled my eyes but then joined in his laughter.

"Fuck you," I said playfully, getting up to go shower. For a moment, I forgot that I'd been in his face looking and smelling like a hot ass mess. I hope he really meant it when he said that he would be there for me, because I needed that kind of support now more than ever.

Antonia

"Would you bring yo slow ass on? We gon' be late because of you," I said fussing at LaCorsha. We were getting ready to go to her first doctor's appointment and check on the baby, find out the due date, etc. I had been on her about going to the doctor to get the baby checked out since we first found out she was pregnant which was a little over a month ago, but she kept making excuses. Finally, I took matters into my own hands and forced her to make an appointment while I was sitting right there. She was so quick to tell me she was pregnant but didn't want to make an appointment to make sure everything was ok. Shit just didn't make sense to me, but I was going to nip that shit in the bud.

"I'm coming, damn! Stop rushing me," Co said coming down the steps. As much as she got on my nerves, I couldn't deny the attraction that I had to her. Once she grabbed her purse and keys, we jumped into the car and headed to the OB/GYN, which was about fifteen to twenty minutes away. It didn't take too long for LaCorsha's name to be called.

Once we got in the examination room and sat up on the table/bed looking thing, we waited for another ten minutes in comfortable silence before the doctor came in.

"Hello Ms. Williams, how are you doing? Dad, I assume?" she asked. Her voice was warm and inviting. I nodded my head and shook her hand.

"I'm good Dr. Hyram, how are you?" LaCorsha asked. The doctor went over to the sink and washed her hands.

"I'm doing good. Let's take a look at this baby, shall we?" she said and we both nodded. She lifted up LaCorsha's shirt. "I'm about to place some gel on your stomach. It may be cold, ok?" she said and LaCorsha nodded to let her know she understood. The doctor grabbed a plastic bottle and squirted some gel on her. She took a little device and used it to rub the gel over her stomach.

"Do you remember your last period?" the doctor asked LaCorsha. LaCorsha gave her the date of her last period and the doctor nodded her head. I kind of tuned them out from the small talk until I heard the distinct sound of a heartbeat. I looked up from my phone and tried to figure out what was going on. "That sound you hear is the baby's heartbeat."

"Oh my God!" LaCorsha said with tears in her eyes. I stood up and walked over to her.

"Where's the baby?" I asked. The doctor pointed me to a tiny little speck.

"Right there. Pretty strong heartbeat already. Looks like you're about twelve weeks, so you'll be due December fifteenth," she said, and we nodded our heads.

"I can't believe we're having a baby," I said. I guess it was finally sinking in. I wanted my kid to be in a two-parent household, where the parents actually liked, loved and respected each other. I had love for Co, I wasn't' in love yet, but that didn't matter. I wanted to make it work with her. The doctor finished up with Co and then left out of the room.

"No, I know I've been on some bullshit with everything going on with work and Talayah and all this other shit, but now that you're carrying my seed, I don't want to stress you out or nothing. I want to be there for you and I want to try to make it work if you're willing to do the same?" I expressed being honest. I expected her to be ecstatic, but instead she gave me a look that I couldn't really read.

"So now that you've decided you don't want to fuck with Talayah or she don't wanna fuck with you then you want to settle for me? If that's what this is then I don't want it. You can't play with my emotions like that Antonio. You've been staying at my house and I can't say that I haven't been enjoying it, but if we're going to do this, then we both need to be one hundred percent. I'm not some fucking rebound, side chick or whatever the fuck you may think. I deserve love and respect like every fucking body else.

If you're just here because you're not with her anymore then you don't need to be with me Antonio and I'm not playing. I will never keep you away from your kid though, I'm not cut like that," she said, and I nodded my head.

"I ain't gon play with you Co. I wouldn't have said that shit if I didn't mean it," I told her.

"We'll see," she said, and we walked out of the office. "Can we go get food? I'm starving," she said.

"Yo fat ass always starving," I joked, and she rolled her eyes. "What you want to eat baby mama?" I asked and she smirked.

"I want crab legs. Let's go to that all you can eat crab spot," she said, and I shook my head. Co was greedy as fuck, but I guess it went in all the right places. I took her out to eat and then we went back to the house and chilled. I can't believe I was about to be a Dad. I never saw that shit for myself. I didn't think I would ever be a family type of man. I never really had a plan, but I'm gonna have to think of more than just myself now.

Yasir

Ever since Talayah opened up to me that night at her house, we been stuck like glue and I can't say I was upset about it. I loved being around her. She brought out a side of me that I really only showed my Mama, and that was saying a lot. I've opened up to her the way I never have with another female and I really liked her.

That story that she told me about her bitch ass ex had me wanting to put that nigga six feet under. He really beat her ass and then left her for dead. If she hadn't called me, then what would have happened to her? Nobody would have been there to take her to the hospital and get her checked out.

Talayah didn't know it but I was going to find out who that nigga was and when I got ahold of him, it was a wrap. What kind of weak ass nigga goes around putting his hands-on females? Especially a female like Talayah. From what she's told me she held that nigga down and all he could do was shit on her over and over again. That shit ain't love. Granted, I'm not a perfect nigga, but I am a real one. If I'm not feeling a female, I let it be known. If I just want to fuck, I let that be known to. Renae is a classic example of that. Yeah, I kept her around for a while and I fucked with her heavy but I tried my best to never lead her on and make her think that what I said and how I acted were two different things.

"What are you thinking about?" Talayah asked breaking me out of my thoughts. We were sitting on her couch just shooting the shit. It felt good to be stress free. She had just been cleared to take the sling off since she only had a minor sprain, which we were both grateful for since I know he stomped on her fucking arm. Just thinking about that shit had me wanting to kill his ass.

I looked over at Talayah and smiled. She was like a breath of fresh air for me. I know she had some shit that came with her, and

I did too, but I didn't give a fuck about all of that. Whatever issues she had I would do my best to help her deal with. I don't know why, but I wanted to protect her, keep her safe, and maybe even love her ass.

"Nothing much. I'm about to go check on my Mom, you wanna come with me?" I asked her.

"You want me to meet your Mom?' she asked and gave me a look.

"Yeah, why not?"

"Won't she think that this is something that it's not?" she asked and it was my turn to give her a look.

"What you mean by something that it's not?"

"I'm just saying, won't she think we're dating?"

"Aren't we dating?"

"I thought we were just taking it slow right now. We're friends," she said, and I was lowkey crushed. She just friend-zoned the fuck out of me.

"Yeah, we friends fasho. Are you coming or not?" I asked standing up. She opened her mouth but then closed it again.

"Yeah I'm coming. Let me go put on some shoes and grab my purse," she said, and I nodded. Her saying that we were just friends made me feel some type of way, but I guess I shouldn't. We haven't really established anything so I couldn't be mad at her for wanting to take things slow. Plus, she just got out of a fucked-up relationship so I had to understand. A few minutes later, she was ready, so we got into the car and headed to my Mom's in an awkward silence.

"Yasir, I'm sorry if I made you feel some type of way when I said we were friends, but we are right? I mean, we haven't made anything official and you know about my last relationship," she said, and I nodded my head.

"It's cool Talayah. I know we've been kicking it and everything and you just got out of a situation so it's cool. I just thought we were working towards something but I'm not gonna be in my feelings about it or no shit like that," I told her.

"We are. I really like you and I believe you really like me too.

We have so much fun together and I do feel like we're building towards something, but I don't want to rush it. I want to take my time with this. You're already like my best friend and I don't want to ruin that by rushing into a relationship. I'm not perfect at all, but I try to be the best person that I can be," she said to me. I had to respect her for being honest. I grabbed her hand and kissed it.

"You got it. I told you I got you and I meant it. Whatever you want, I'm with it," I said, and she smiled. I kissed the back of her hand and then pulled off towards my Mom's house.

About ten minutes later, we pulled up to my Mom's home. She lived in a beautiful two story, four bedroom and two-bathroom house in Troy, MI, about five minutes away from Somerset mall. Til this day I think she chose this house on purpose because she loves to shop. I pulled up to the house, parked in the driveway and was just about to get out until Talayah grabbed my arm. I looked at her and she had a terrified expression on her face.

"I'm scared," she said shyly.

"What you scared for?" I asked and she didn't answer. "You scared of my Mama?" Again, she didn't say a word, just nodded her head. I chuckled. She looked so cute and innocent right now. "Girl she ain't nobody to be scared of, relax. She'll love you," I said and hopped out of the car before she could get another word out. I waited a few moments and Talayah came out of the car. We walked up to the door and I used my key to get in.

"Who is that?!" I heard my Mom yelling from the kitchen. I chuckled and made my way through the foyer, down the hall and to the kitchen.

"Let me find out somebody else got a key to yo house," I told her, and she turned around smiling.

"If they did, that's my damn business," she said kissing me on my cheek. She looked over at Talayah, and smiled. "Well, who is this Yasir?" she asked and I looked over at Talayah who looked like she was about to shit bricks. It was taking everything in me not to laugh at her.

"This, is my friend Talayah. Talayah, this is my Mom, Ms. Lynda Fuller, everybody either calls her Ms. Lynda or Mama Lyn," I told Talayah.

"Nice to meet you Ms. Fuller," Talayah said stretching her hand out for my Mom to shake.

"Oh I don't do handshakes baby. Give me a hug," my Mom said smiling, pulling Talayah in for a hug. "And you don't have to be so formal, you can call me Mama Lyn," she said and Talayah shook her head. "Are you hungry?" she asked us and I shook my head yes. I really wasn't hungry, but I'll eat whatever my Mama cooked. She could burn in the kitchen.

"I'm not really hungry right now, but thank you for the offer," Talayah said and I looked at her.

"Lay, let me let you in on something. If she offers you something to eat, you say yes. She's old school so she takes it as a sign of disrespect if you turn down her cooking," I said taking a seat at the kitchen table.

"Oh, I'm sorry," Talayah said shyly. I could tell she was nervous as fuck and I thought it was cute. She really didn't have a reason to be. My Mom was the sweetest lady you'll ever meet until you pissed her off or messed with her kids, then it was an issue. I have to say in all twenty-eight of my years on this earth, I can count on my hands how many times I've witnessed my Mom get angry or yell her voice. She was always so cool and that's what I loved about her.

"Relax," I whispered in Talayah's ear as she sat down next to me at the kitchen table. We ate and made small talk, and they both seemed to warm up to each other as some time passed. I could literally see the tension leaving Talayah's body.

"So, I assume you got rid of that whore you were messing around with?" my Mom asked. We had finished eating and were now in the living room just watching tv and chilling.

"Ma, what whore you talking about?" I asked chuckling. I knew exactly who she was talking about, but I wanted to hear her say it.

"Oh, you got so many that you don't know which one I'm talking about?" she asked. I looked at Talayah, who was already looking at me.

"Don't look at me, inquiring minds wanna know," she said folding her arms and playfully rolling her neck. I chuckled and she giggled in return.

"Man, who you talkin' 'bout Ma?" I asked.

"That Renae girl," she confirmed.

"Nah, I'm not rocking with Renae no more," I said honestly.

"Thank God. I can't stand that tramp," she said and Talayah bust out laughing.

"What did she do Mama Lyn?" Talayah asked being nosey.

"She just rubs me the wrong way. She tries too hard to get Yasir to love her," my Mom said and Talayah nodded her head like she understood. "I ain't never begged no man to give a fuck about me. It's desperate. The woman should always be the catch, not the other way around. Men like when you make them work for your love," she said looking over at Talayah. "Never, and I mean never make him think that your love is to be taken as a joke or that it can be easily obtained. When something comes to easy, they don't want it anymore and they'll throw you out with the trash. You are not trash, I can tell. You ain't like all these other young bitches walking around here trying to catch a man. You've only told me a little bit about yourself but I know you have your head on right. You're a queen and you don't ever forget that and don't allow your crown to tip or fall off your pretty little head. You hear me?" she said. I looked over at Talayah who had tears coming down her face. I've never heard her talk so highly of somebody that I've dated, but then again, I've only bought Renae and my first girlfriend in high school to meet my Mom.

"I hear you Mama Lyn," she said wiping her tears. I felt a little awkward in this moment, and I wanted to excuse myself but it would be rude as fuck to get up right now.

"Enough of all that crying now. I was going to ask why your arm is in this sling and your face all bruised up, but that's not my business. But I need you to tell me something," she said looking over at me.

"Wassup Ma?"

"Are y'all really just friends or are y'all boning?" she asked.

Talayah and I glanced at each other and then busted out laughing.

"Man, naw Ma. We're not," I told her. She looked skeptical but didn't press the issue any further. We stayed at my Mom's house a few more minutes before finally leaving. On the ride home, Talayah was extremely quiet, like she was in deep thought.

"What's on your mind baby girl?" I asked.

"Just thinking. I've never connected with someone's Mom like that. Literally, never. It feels like I've been around her for years," she expressed, and I smiled. I'm glad they liked each other.

"That's good. I'm glad that you feel close to her. You need to know that you have people around you who care about you."

"I do have people, I've got Beanie, Giselle and my Mom. Even though I don't really talk to my Mom, I know she cares," she said.

"Well, feel free to use my Mama anytime," I said smiling. It seemed like she was doing better since that day she was crying her eyes out over her bitch ass ex. I couldn't wait to get my hands on him. We were just pulling up to her house when my phone started ringing. For a split second, I forgot that my car was hooked up to Bluetooth, which made the whole car ring. I looked at the screen on my dashboard and frowned. I hit ignore, parked and got out of the car.

"Why'd you ignore her?" Talayah asked once we got in the house.

"Because she doesn't want shit and I'm not about to give her the satisfaction of hearing my voice," I said sternly.

"Alright mean ass," she said holding her hands up in mock surrender. She walked off towards the steps and I collapsed on the couch to watch TV. Not even five minutes after I sat down, my phone was vibrating again. I dug the phone out of my pocket and looked at the screen. Renae was calling yet again. I thought she was cool with us severing whatever it was she thought we had, but I could see now she was going to be a fucking problem, but I wouldn't let her fuck up what I was trying to build with Lay. She was already mine whether she wanted to admit it or not. All I had to do was make it official, and I planned on doing that real soon.

Talayah

Lately, I've been high off life and I can't say that I wasn't loving it. Business was booming, my friends and family were good and my love life was blossoming. My bruises healed and my arm was out of the sling.

Yasir and I spent all of our free time together and as much as I hate to admit it, I was falling for him. We hadn't had sex yet and I was happy that he wasn't rushing it. He was really taking his time to get to know me and show me that he wasn't like all these other niggas out here. He gave me a different vibe that I didn't want to go away anytime soon.

"What you over there smiling for?" Giselle asked. We were currently at my house having a girls' day, eating junk food, watching Netflix and just relaxing. We always tried to have this time for each other at least once a month.

"Nothing," I said feeling myself blushing.

"You a nothing lie. Let me find out," she teased.

"Okay, fine, I'm lying. I'm just thinking about how lit life is right now. I don't have any complaints. Everything is going good with the shop, my bills are all paid, I haven't seen or heard from Antonio's ass in a few weeks and Yasir been making a bitch feel like she's the shit!" I explained with a big smile on my face.

"Oh, bitch y'all been fucking," she said, and I laughed.

"No, we haven't. Not yet," I said, and her eyes grew wide.

"So you mean to tell me that y'all have been spending all this time together and he ain't even sniffed the pussy?" she asked and I playfully rolled my eyes.

"No bitch! Just because you would be busting it open by now doesn't mean I have to. It's not about sex with us at all. We have a deeper connection," I told her.

"Alright deep connection, he needs to be deep in them guts!" she said laughing and I couldn't help but to join her.

"It'll happen when it's supposed to, I'm not going to rush. I really like him, and I don't want anything to ruin it," I told her, and she nodded.

"I get that bestie. If he makes you happy then I'm more than happy for you. I never thought I'd see the day that you actually moved on from Antonio so I'm beyond proud," she said, and I nodded.

"Me either," I said, my mind drifting back to my relationship with Antonio. I've never felt more low and stupid in my life. He made me feel like I wasn't good enough, like I wasn't worthy of a man loving me the right way and I'll be damned if I ever let that happen again.

"Don't get in your feelings about his ass Lay. You've been doing good," she said reaching over and patting my leg. I was just about to respond to her when my phone vibrated. I looked at the screen and smiled. Yasir just texted me.

Yasir: *Do you have plans a little later?*
Me: *No, just kicking it with Giselle. Wassup?*
Yasir: *Oh, I don't want to take you away from your girl*
Me: *It's fine. Wassup?*
Yasir: *I wanna take you out to eat. I know you hungry*
Me: *Lol. U tryna be funny? Is this a date?*
Yasir: *Hell yeah it is*

I laughed at that text message. My greedy ass was always hungry. I agreed to let him take me out and then got up from the couch to find something to wear.

"Where are you going?" Giselle asked. I ignored her as I continued to my room. I went to my closet and started looking through clothes. "Bitch I know you hear me talking to you!"

"I don't have anything to wear!" I screamed.

"Wear for what? Where are you going?" she asked again.

"Yasir is coming to get me in a couple of hours and we're going out to eat," I said excitedly.

"Bitch are you twelve?" she said smiling. "You this excited

about going out to eat with Yasir? Don't y'all always go out to eat?" she asked.

"Not really. We mostly just hang out at each other's houses, relax and talk," I said.

"Oh, so this is like a date?" she asked and I nodded. "Okay bitch let me see what you've got!" she said going to sit on my bed.

Ten minutes later, we'd picked out the perfect outfit. It was simple but cute as hell; a nude bodysuit with long sleeves, ripped black skinny jeans and a nude heel. I took a quick shower, curled my hair and had Giselle do my make-up. She wasn't a make-up artist, but she could beat a face. Once she was done, I looked in my full-length mirror admiring myself.

"Walking past the mirror, oh! Damn I'm fine!" I said singing Cardi B. Giselle laughed.

"Yas bitch! Ya look good! Ya look blessed!" she said quoting Kendall Kyndall from Instagram. We both laughed. Just as I was putting all my stuff in my black Louis Vuitton hand bag, my phone rang. It was Yasir letting me know he was outside.

"Alright so he's outside," I told her. I left out of the house and got into his car.

"You look good as fuck," he said licking his lips at me. I looked over at him and damn he looked good as fuck. He was wearing all black with a single Cuban link chain around his neck. I noticed he had on a gold watch to match and his smooth dark chocolate skin was doing something to me. His full lips made it hard for me to not kiss him and his beard made me want to sit on his face.

"Thank you. You look good yourself," I said, and he pulled off.

"So, where are we going?" I asked.

"*Ruth Chris*. Have you ever been?" he asked me.

"No, I never have."

"You'll love the steak," he told me, and I got excited.

"I love steak!" I exclaimed.

"Yeah I know you do greedy ass," he said chuckling and I chuckled as well. Yasir turned the volume up on the radio and we cruised down I-75 singing every song that came on. We were really like best friends, and it scared me to take it to that next level. I didn't want to ruin everything, but I definitely wanted us to be together, I just didn't know if he felt the same way. I'm not saying anything though, I'll just go with the flow.

We walked into the restaurant and were seated rather quickly. The vibe in the restaurant was very romantic. The elevator music, the low lights with the candles lit at every table and the fancy china that everyone was eating on made me fall in love. Yasir ordered a bottle of champagne and shortly after our waiter came to take our orders.

"This is a fancy place Yasir," I said smiling.

"You deserve fancy, don't you think?" he asked and I shrugged.

"Don't do that. You deserve that and then some," he said grabbing my hand and kissing it. His lips on my skin made me moist between my legs. I looked at him and blushed.

"Thank you. You're always so sweet to me."

"I try," he said winking. "So, I want to run something by you that's been going on at work. Business owner to business owner," he said to me and I nodded my head.

"What's going on?"

"Well, one of my employees came to me a while back and told me that my management team is lacking some of the key qualities needed to run a team," he said, and my face scrunched up.

"Qualities like what?"

"Well, he wasn't very clear, so I took that as a hint to see for myself, and I have been keeping a pretty close eye on my management staff and there's this one guy, Lance that has been pissing me off. When I initially gave him the position, he was doing great, but I think he's gotten too comfortable which is causing his performance as a manager to become piss poor," he told me, and I nodded my head. I knew all too well how that could be.

"I know what you mean. I originally had a shop manager at *Black Girl Magic.* She was one of my closest friends and a great business woman, but I think that because she was my closest friend, she started power tripping. She started doing whatever the fuck she wanted to do and the shop was not in a good space. I had to make a decision that could have ruined either my shop or my friendship. I chose to let her go, and it honestly made both my business and our friendship stronger," I explained.

"Well, I wouldn't say Lance and I were best friends but he's been an outstanding an employee up until recently. I don't know if I want to fire him, demote him or just put him on probation," he said.

"I say if your employees under this guy are having an issue then cut out the cancer all together. No need to prolong it," I told him, and he nodded.

"I knew I could come to you. You give good advice," he said, and I smiled.

"I try. I wish I knew how to take my own advice sometimes, it's just..." I started to say but Yasir's phone started to ring on the table. I looked at him and watched as he rolled his eyes. An uneasy feeling came over me. I knew that no bitch would be calling him over and over like this if she didn't have a reason or feel like she could. He ignored the phone call and then looked at me.

"I'm sorry about that," he said, and I waved him off.

"Don't worry about it. I know how it is," I told him, and he nodded his head. He opened his mouth to say something but was cut off by someone calling his name.

"Really Yasir? You're really just going to ignore my phone call? I don't care about you being out on a date or whatever this is," the voice said. I looked at Yasir who's nostrils were flared, and hands balled into a fist. I then looked up at the girl and instantly recognized her as the chick whose hair I did on Yasir's birthday. I rolled my eyes.

"Bitch is there a problem?" she asked rolling her neck and folding her arms under her breast. I mugged her.

"If I was you, I'd watch that bitch word. I'm not the one lil mama. I promise you don't want no smoke. You remember what happened last time" I told her and then turned my attention to the menu. I wasn't trying to cause a scene in this place. Everybody was already staring at us due to her loud ass mouth. I heard Yasir going back and forth with her, but I drowned it out up until I heard her disrespect me again.

"You know what? Fuck you and this bitch. Y'all can have each other," she shouted. I started to get up but Yasir looked at me.

"Don't even do it. You got too much to lose to be fighting with some bird ass bitch," he said, and I nodded my head and sat back down smirking at the chick.

"Bird ass bitch? Nigga, you got me fucked up!" she said and raised her hand to swing but Yasir caught her wrist.

"You causing a hell of a scene. I done told you before, you ain't my bitch. I don't belong to you. I can take out whoever the fuck I wanna take out and you can't say shit about it. I told you whatever we had was dead and I meant that shit. You got one more time to come at me or her sideways and I promise I'll come after you and everybody you love," he said through gritted teeth. His voice was calm and authoritative, and it was sexy as hell seeing him handling her the way he was. I crossed my legs and squeezed them together under the table to stop the try and stop the tingling feeling I was getting between my legs.

I along with the other people around me couldn't tear my eyes away from the scene that was unfolding before us. I just knew Renae was going to jump stupid, but instead, she sucked her teeth and snatched away from Yasir.

"This," she started, pointing between her and Yasir "ain't over," she snarled and then stormed out of the restaurant. A few of the tables next to us looked at Yasir for a few more moments before going back to their meals. Yasir sat back down in his chair and rubbed his hand over his face.

"I'm so sorry about that Talayah. I didn't mean for you to see me get out of character. I'm just so sick of her ass. How many times can you tell a person no?" he asked blowing out a frustrated breath. I reached over and placed my hand over his.

"Don't worry about it, I can handle that…" I started to say but I felt a pair of eyes on me. Breaking eye contact with Yasir, I looked around the restaurant and finally my eyes landed on the last person I expected to see.

"What's wrong?" he asked but I couldn't respond all I could do was stare off into space and try to remain calm and in my seat.

"Can we go?" I asked.

"Go? We haven't ordered or gotten our food yet. What's wrong? What or who did you just see?" he said trying to turn around and see what had me shook. I quickly leaped out of my seat and grabbed his shoulders.

"No!" I shouted. "It was nothing. I just feel like we've already caused a scene and I'm kind of embarrassed with all these white folks looking at us like we're beneath them," I said in a hushed tone. He looked at me as if he knew I was lying but didn't object. He got up, grabbed my hand and escorted me out of the restaurant. Once we reached the parking lot, I blew out a breath I hadn't realized I was holding in. Tonight couldn't have been any worse.

Antonio

The last few months have been going pretty well, I couldn't even complain. I missed the hell out of Talayah, but I tried my hardest to redirect my energy onto LaCorsha. It was difficult, but I really was making an effort and I could tell that she was as well.

She's really been trying to be the perfect woman for me and I appreciated her for it. We were working towards something and I liked it. I would've liked it better had it been with Talayah, but like I said, I was working on pushing her to the back of my mind. Deep down, I knew I was settling but it felt like there was nothing that I could do about it without losing my mind.

"What are you thinking about?" Co asked breaking me out of my thoughts.

"I'm just thinking about the baby. I'm ready to find out what it is," I half lied. I was ready to find out about the baby but I wasn't about to tell her I was thinking about Talayah. One thing I've learned is that you don't piss off the pregnant lady.

"Me too. We will in a few hours," she said excitedly. We both finished getting dressed and then hopped in the car to go to LaCorsha's appointment. I was hoping for a mini me but of course she wanted a baby girl. I don't think I could handle having a girl. I would have to shoot every teenage boy she thought she might like because I knew she would be drop dead gorgeous. My son, on the other hand, I could handle. I would raise him to be better than I could have ever been.

Once we got to the OB/GYN, we signed in and sat in the waiting room. I looked around at a few other pregnant women and noticed that they were alone. I grabbed LaCorsha's hand and lightly squeezed it. She looked at me, smiled and then pecked my lips. I really didn't want her to ever have to go through this alone.

I was going to be there for her and my baby no matter what, together or not. I would rather have us together though. My kid deserved to be in a healthy, loving, two parent household, which is something that neither one of us had growing up. As fucked up as I knew I could be, I did care for Co. It's just that my heart still belonged to someone else Now that I think about it, I kind of sounded like I was only with her for the sake of my kid, but I really did fuck with her heavy. I wasn't in love, but I had genuine feelings for her that could one day turn into love.

We were called to the back and LaCorsha laid on the table. I looked at her belly that seemed to be growing every day, and smiled as she rubbed it.

"I can't wait to find out what this baby is so we can start shopping," she said.

"You tryna spend all my money already?" I teased and she smacked her lips.

"Yours and mine. Let's not forget that I have my own. Yours is just extra," she stated, and I nodded my head. That's one of the reasons why I fucked with her, she didn't need a nigga for shit. That's what attracted me to her in the first place.

"Alright Mom and Dad, are we ready to see if little peanut will like Barbie's or action figures?" the doctor said as she came into the room.

"Yeah, we're ready Doc," I told her.

"More than ready," Co responded. Co lifted her shirt up while the doctor washed her hands and prepared for the ultrasound. She squeezed the gel on her belly and used the tool to move the gel all over her stomach. I instantly heard my baby's heartbeat and it was like music to my ears. After a few minutes, she said those few words that we'd been waiting to hear.

"Alright, it looks like our little peanut has a penis!" she said and I jumped up.

"Hell yeah!" I yelled with excitement.

"Aww man now I owe him twenty dollars," LaCorsha said sounding a little disappointed.

"I'm sorry baby I know you wanted a girl, but now you have

to deal with two of me foreva," I said mocking Cardi B and she laughed.

"Forever, huh?" she asked and I realized what I just said.

"Something like that," I said smirking. I bent down and kissed her and then kissed her belly.

"My little man," I said kissing her belly over and over. I stopped kissing long enough to let the doctor take a look at the baby, wipe the gel off of her belly and schedule her next appointment.

"Well, now we can go shopping," she said excitedly. "I'm happy we're having a boy, but I definitely would've been happier with a girl," she said pouting.

"You'll be ok," I said sticking my tongue out at her.

"Can we go eat before we go shopping? Me and AJ are hungry?" she asked and I gave her a look.

"You want to name him after me?" I said, slightly shocked. We hadn't had the talk about names yet.

"Yes, why not? He is your son," she said nonchalantly. Tears formed in my eyes and I tried to wipe them away before they ran down my cheeks. "Awww look at you. I've never seen you so emotional," she said grabbing my cheeks and kissing my lips.

"That's because nothing can ever bring out emotions like your kid," I told her, and she nodded. I can't believe I was about to have a Junior.

"It's very sexy on you, Daddy," she said kissing me again, this time more passionately.

"Are you really tryna fuck in the doctor's office?" I asked smirking at her. She didn't respond, just nodded her head.

"Freaky ass," I said grabbing her breasts. That's another thing I loved about Co, she wanted to get it in any and everywhere. Talayah's ass would never be down for no shit like this.

Co reached for my pants and slid them down, which was easy to do since I had on jogging pants. I grabbed her ankles and slid her down a little bit, taking off her leggings. I slid her panties to the side and flicked my tongue over her clit.

"Aah," she moaned. I used my index fingers to spread her

lips apart and inserted my tongue in her center, going in a circular motion. I knew she liked when I did that. "Fuck!" she yelled. I continued to please her with my tongue and then inserted two fingers in her. She really went crazy then. I loved hearing her moan. It made my dick hard. "Baby I can't take it anymore, please give it to me," she begged. I smirked at her and pulled out my dick.

"Is this what you want?" I asked gently rubbing my dick against her opening.

"Now Antonio," she said a little more forcefully.

"Yo pregnant ass is bossy as fuck, you know that, right?"

"I'm pregnant, horny and hungry. Give me what I want before I go in your shit," she said threatening me.

"So violent," I said entering her. I slowly went in and out of her, further teasing her. I know Co liked to fuck and not make love, especially when she really wanted to get a nut off.

"Antonio stop playing with me," she said breathing heavily. Finally, I gave her what she wanted and started pounding into her. Gentle, yet forceful at the same time. She was weird like that, but it was kind of sexy.

"Fuck," I moaned. Whoever said pregnant pussy was the wettest pussy was absolutely right. Co's pussy felt like a fucking ocean wrapped around my dick. It was so hard for me to not cum quickly, but I wanted her to get off before I did.

"Yes Tony. You feel so good," she whined, which only made me go harder. I continue to pound into her until she released on my dick. I came right after her. I slowly pulled out and then rinsed my dick off at the sink. I looked in the cabinets and found a wash rag and wet it with warm water and soap and used it to clean her up. Once we were both dressed, we headed out of the doctor's office.

"I feel like everybody's looking at us," she whispered to me.

"They probably heard yo loud ass," I said laughing and she playfully punched me in the arm. "Don't be embarrassed, yo freaky ass wanted it. Now come on freak, let's go get you some food and go shop for our boy," I said rubbing her belly. Since we were already close to the mall, we decided to go there first.

LaCorsha shopped until she literally couldn't shop anymore. She made sure that she got all the shit I didn't like, but it's ok, I would go out and get my boy some fly shit on my own. We got to the mall around three-thirty pm and by the time we were ready to leave it was almost seven pm. LaCorsha was starving by then, so I decided to take her to *Ruth Chris*. I knew she would fuck some steak up.

We were seated, placed our orders and had casual conversation. I stared in her big brown eyes and smiled. She looked so happy and she had a glow on her face, which I knew was because of the baby.

"Why are you looking at me like that?" she asked. "I got a booger in my nose or something?"

"No, you look beautiful and I'm happy that you're carrying my son," I told her, and she gave me a wide smile.

"Thanks Antonio. I know sometimes you wish she was having your kid instead of me, but I can see that you're really trying to make this work and I really appreciate that Tony," she told me. I could see a wave of sadness wash over her, but she tried to play it off. The waitress came with our food and we began eating before I responded.

"It's not that I wish it was her instead of you, it's just that I always thought we'd get it together, get over the hump, you know? I always thought that she would be the one but..." I said but stopped midsentence. I looked up and locked eyes with Talayah.

"But what?" I heard LaCorsha say, but I couldn't answer her. It was like all common sense went out the window when my eyes connected with Talayah. She looked good as fuck with her hair curled the way that it was. I was looking at her with lust and love in my eyes, but she was looking at me as if she'd seen a ghost; or worse, the devil.

My eyes stay connected with hers for what felt like a while until she tore her eyes away from mine. She mouthed something to somebody and that's when I noticed that she was with someone else, and judging by the back of the person's head, it was a man. Anger shot through my body. She moved on already or was she fucking this nigga behind my back the whole time?

Just as I was about to get up and go over there and speak my mind, they got up and left. I couldn't see the dudes face, but best believe I was going to find out. Whoever that nigga was, he was going to feel me. I don't give a fuck what I did, but Talayah would always be mine. Yes, I know I just said I was accepting my situation and moving forward, but fuck that. Talayah had me fucked up if she thought I was just going to let her move on.

After they left, I finally focused my attention back on LaCorsha who looked like she wanted to slap the shit out of me.

"Are you done staring?" she asked with an attitude.

"Man get the fuck on with that bullshit Co," I said waving her off. Deep down, I knew I was in the wrong but I didn't feel like explaining myself or arguing with her.

"Wow," she said throwing her fork and knife on her plate and sitting back in her chair with her arms folded.

"I guess you got an attitude now?" I asked and she didn't respond. "Alright then let's just pack this shit up and go home," I said flagging the waiter down.

She looked like she wanted to protest but decided against it. Instead, she sucked her teeth but didn't say anything back, which I was grateful for. I was going to have to go upside her fucking head if she caused a scene in this restaurant. I wasn't in the mood to be going back and forth with her ass. They brought to-go boxes, I paid the tab and we left.

The ride home was silent, but I couldn't say I gave a fuck. When we got home, she jumped out of the car before I could even come to a complete stop. I chuckled at her being mad and decided to give Talayah a piece of my mind.

Me: So you found yourself a new nigga?

Lay Lay: Don't text my phone trying to check me. Matter of fact, you can keep on texting, but you'll be talking to yourself. Fuck you and have a nice day.

Me: Bitch who you think you talking to?

Me: You got me fucked up if you think I'm about to sit back and let you be with some weak ass nigga.

Me: I'm coming for you Lay Lay. You're mine until I don't want your ass anymore.

I waited a few minutes to see if she'd respond, but I realized that she blocked me. She really had moved on like I never meant shit to her, but it was alright, because I had something for her.
• •

A week later

"Antonio!" I heard someone shout from across the room. I looked up to see who was calling me and noticed my supervisor, Lance headed towards me. I took off my protective goggles and met him halfway.

"What's going on?" I asked.

"Mr. White wants to speak with you. Follow me," he said with a smirk. I wondered what Mr. White wanted to speak with me about? I haven't seen or spoken to him since the day I told him about this lazy son of a bitch in front of me. *Oh shit!* I thought. *What if he's about to fire my dumb ass?* Lance's fat ass would love to get rid of me. He knew I wanted his job, so he always tried to find ways to get rid of me but came up short. He escorted me to Mr. White's door and then mouthed good luck to me. If it wasn't for the fact that I was at work, I'd punch him dead in his mouth, but I had to remain professional.

"You wanted to see me Mr. White?" I asked and he nodded then extended his hand offering the seat across from the desk.

"Yes, I wanted to talk to you about something. Feel free to call me Yasir," he said, and I nodded.

"So, what is it that you'd like to talk about? Have I done something wrong?" I asked wondering if Lance came and told him a bunch of bullshit.

"No. Nothing like that," he assured me, and I breathed a sigh of relief. "I just wanted to let you know that I've been thinking about the conversation that you and I had and I wanted to let you know that I heard you. With that being said, I would like to offer you a position in management. You seem to know what you're doing and what the team needs out there on the floor, so I think you'd be perfect for the position," he said. It took everything in me not to jump out this chair and shout.

"Thank you so much. I really appreciate the opportunity," I said reaching over to shake his hand.

"Not a problem, I know you'll make me proud," he said.

"So, are you adding a new team to the floor or am I replacing an existing supervisor?" I asked.

"Don't let anyone else know, but you'll be taking Lance's position. Ever since you came to me, I've been watching him and my other employees in management and I haven't seen anybody slacking but him, so I knew you had to be speaking of him," he said, and I nodded.

"I see. Well I thank you again for the opportunity and I promise that you will not regret the decision," I said to him and he smiled.

"I'm sure I won't. In honor of your new-found position, why don't I take you out to celebrate?" he asked and I was shocked.

"I'd love to! When are you free?"

"How about next Friday?"

"Sure, no problem."

"I know you have someone special, why don't you bring her?" he suggested and for a moment, I thought about Talayah, but then remembered that she didn't want shit to do with me. Especially after I saw her with some nigga, and then she blatantly curved me after I confronted her about it. It's fucked up how she's still the first person I think about when I want to tell someone good news. I really had fucked up a good thing, and to make matters even worse, she had the audacity to move on like I wasn't going to come back for her when I was ready.

"Yeah, of course, I definitely will," I told him standing up. We shook hands again and I left out of his office, smiling to myself. I passed Lance on the way back to the line and he gave me a look that I couldn't read. I wanted to respond, but decided not to. He was going to be pissed once he realized the new guy was taking the spot that he worked years to be in and I couldn't be fucking happier. I was going to get the job I deserved and then I was going to get my bitch back.

Yasir

I wanted to ask Talayah what was wrong at *Ruth Chris* last week, but I figured that she'd come and talk to me when she was ready. She looked really scared, like she saw a ghost or something so I didn't want to pressure her and force her to talk about something that would make her uncomfortable.

In the meantime, I had to find a way to get Renae's ass off my fucking back. I thought that I'd already cleared the air on my birthday, but I guess not. She hadn't stopped blowing my phone up since that day, and that was months ago. Not only was it irritating me, I could tell it annoyed Talayah. She never said anything about it, but her energy always changes when she notices her calling. I didn't want her to think that I was still fucking around with her or anybody else for that matter. I wanted to make this thing with us official. I was going to ask at *Ruth Chris*, but our dinner got cut short. I was just going to come out and say it. Sit her down, let her know what it is and go from there. She can either choose to ride with me or not.

"What you in here thinking about babe?" Talayah said coming from behind me and kissing my cheek. I was currently in my office, working from home. I was going to go in, but I didn't feel like it. Perks of being your own boss.

"You as usual," I told her, and she smiled. I loved her smile, and every time I saw it I swear all I wanted to do was keep it there permanently.

"You so cute," she said and then sat on the couch that I had in my office. "I didn't want to disturb you while you're working, I just wanted to be in the same room as you," she said. Now it was my turn to smile.

"Anytime you're around it's a distraction. Have you seen

97

you?" I flirted and I could've sworn that I saw her blush. "So, I did want to speak with you about something a little later if that's cool with you," I expressed.

"Yeah, of course. Is it bad?" she asked sounding a little worried.

"No it's not bad. It's really good. Well in my eyes it is, and I think you'll be happy," I told her, and she smiled and nodded.

"Well okay, I trust you," she said and for some reason that did something to me.

"You do?" I asked.

"Why wouldn't I? You haven't given me a reason not to," she told me, and I swear it felt like I've been blown off of my feet.

"Damn, I haven't heard that in…never," I said honestly.

"Well you're welcome. Look at me, changing your life," she said twirling around and I laughed.

"You silly as hell. I know you gotta go to the shop for a minute, but can you meet me back here around nine pm?"

"Yeah of course. I shouldn't be long. I'm just about to go over the books really quick, nothing major," she told me, and I nodded.

Once she left, I set my plan in motion, I planned to make tonight THE night. I could honestly say that I've never felt the way I feel for Talayah about anyone in my life. I wanted her around me all the time. I know we've only been kicking it for a few months, but I was falling for her ass, hard. She was like my best friend, my business consultant and my girl all wrapped up in one, and I hadn't even gotten the pussy yet. Really, it wasn't about that. Of course, I wanted to feel her and to experience that connection with her, but I know she just got out of an abusive relationship and I wasn't trying to pressure her. I wanted to do the exact opposite of what her bitch ass ex had done and I planned to do that with my actions. I got up from my desk and started to put my plan in motion.

Time always seems to speed up when you've got shit planned out, but I say I was doing pretty well. I managed to cook, light candles, get the rose petals and spread them out, all I was waiting on now was Talayah. I knew she was going to love this. She seemed like the type to love grand romantic gestures. Just as I was plating the food at the kitchen table, I heard the door open. Yes, I gave her a key. I didn't have shit to hide from her. I hurried to meet her at the door before she saw too much.

"What are you up to? And what's that smell? You cooked?" she asked firing off question after question. She looked at me skeptically when she asked if I cooked and I slightly chuckled.

"Why don't you come in the kitchen and see?" I suggested and reached out for her hand. She grabbed my hand and I led her to the kitchen.

"Awww rose petals!" she exclaimed. I'm assuming that she was just now looking down. As we walked into the kitchen, I looked at her and I saw nothing but pure shock.

"You cooked this!?" she exclaimed.

"That's all you focused on?" I joked and she shrugged her shoulders.

"I didn't know you knew how to cook. No man has ever cooked for me before, that's all," she said.

"Well I'm glad I could be the first. Come eat," I told her. I made steak, broccoli with cheese, potatoes and Hawaiian rolls. Who doesn't love Hawaiian rolls? "You want something to drink?" I asked her.

"Just water, thank you," she smiled. I brought her a glass of water and then sat down to enjoy the food.

"This is so good Yasir," she said scarfing down her plate like she hadn't ate all day.

"I'm glad you like it greedy ass girl," I teased. She stuck her tongue out at me and I cleared my throat. I guess now was the best time to let her know how I was feeling.

"So, what did you need to talk to me about?" she asked beating me to the punch.

"As a matter of fact, I was just getting to that," I started. "I know we've only known each other for a few months now, but I swear since the very first moment that I laid eyes on you, all I wanted to do was protect you, and make you smile. You've become my best friend and I swear I ain't never felt this way about a female in my life. I don't know what it is, but I want you around. I want to make you happy and I want to show you that I ain't shit like your bitch ass ex. I can make you happy and keep you happy," I told her.

"So you're saying all that to say what?" she asked.

"I'm saying that to say, you're mine now and I'm not taking no for an answer."

"What if I don't want to be?" she asked, and it threw me off. I couldn't make out if she was serious or not, but I prayed to God she was just playing with me.

"You don't?"

"I do, I just wanted to see you sweat a little bit," she laughed, and I breathed a sigh of relief.

"I was about to say."

"You weren't about to say shit," she teased as she finished her plate. "That was delicious, and thank you for everything. I didn't want to rush it, but it feels good to know that you feel the same way about me that I feel about you," she said, and I reached for her hand and grabbed it.

"Come on, I got something else for you," I said, helping her up from the table and leading her up the stairs. We got to the bedroom that was damn near covered in rose petals.

"This is so beautiful Yasir," she said kissing my lips.

"I got a hot bath running for you. Go ahead and relax and I'll be right here waiting on you," I told her.

"Or, you could get in with me," she said seductively.

"Are you sure you're ready?" I asked. "I don't want you to think that I did all of this just to get some pussy. I really do want to be with you. All of you," I said sincerely.

"I know, and that's why I want to give you all of me. Right here, right now. So, come on," she said disappearing into the bathroom. I quickly hopped off the bed and went into the bathroom. We looked at each other for a while and I leaned down to kiss her passionately. Never removing her lips from hers, I managed to take her shirt and bra off. She took off her jeans and underwear and I swear I was mesmerized. Yes, we'd been sleeping in the same bed almost every night, but I've never gotten the pleasure to see her naked. I felt like I was looking at a goddess.

"You're so fucking beautiful," I told her, removing my own clothing. After I came out of my underwear, I noticed her staring at my third leg.

"You like what you see?" I asked seductively.

"It looks like a big ass milky way or snickers bar. It's so pretty," she said innocently.

"Did you just call my dick pretty?" I laughed. "I ain't never heard that before."

"I don't know how else to put it," she shrugged and then got in the tub. I joined her. We spent our time in the tub exploring each other for the first time. I swear I was on a high like no other. We washed each other up and then I carried her from the tub onto the bed. I dried her off and bent down to kiss her again. I started at her lips, down to her neck, sucking slowly on her perfectly round breasts. I made my way her down to her stomach and finally, my lips met her center. As soon as I licked her clit, I felt her whole-body shiver.

"Oh my God!" she moaned in pleasure. I circled her clit over and over like I was licking an ice cream cone.

"Yes Yasir, right there baby," she said using her hands to guide my head. I lifted her legs so that they were wrapped around my legs and then quickly flipped her over so that she was straddling my face. She rode me for a few moments and then I felt her legs start to shake.

"Damn baby I'm cumming!" she said and I smiled on the inside. She came in my mouth and I swear it was the sweetest taste ever, like a piece of cherry candy. She got off of my face and then slid down to my dick.

"What you doing Lay?" I asked her.

"You made me feel good, I'm returning the favor," she said wrapping her mouth around my dick. The warm sensation made me moan out like a bitch, but I didn't care. She slowly worked her tongue around my pole, up and down and then around in circles.

"Damn baby," I said in pleasure.

"You like that?" she asked never removing her mouth from my shaft.

"Fuck yeah," I told her guiding her head. She lifted up and spit on my dick and went back to work. Within a few minutes, I felt my nut building up.

"Lift up baby, lift up," I said not wanting to cum in her mouth. She lifted up and I was grateful.

"What's wrong?" she asked.

"Nothing, I didn't want to cum in your mouth," I told her.

"Why not?" she asked, and I gave her a confused look.

"What do you mean why? I don't want to feel like I'm disrespecting you. I do that shit to hoes not to my girl," I said, and she shrugged.

"If you ask me, your girl should be your hoe too. That way you don't have use for none of these other bitches," she said, and I smirked.

"You think you know something," I told her grabbing her waist and lifting her up and then down on my dick.

"Ahh, I guess you can say that," she moaned. For the rest of the night we explored each other's bodies until we couldn't take it anymore and fell asleep.

The next morning, I woke up and Talayah wasn't in the bed. I figured she must have gone to the shop or something until I smelled the distinct smell of bacon frying. I hopped out of the bed, put on some boxers and headed downstairs to see what Talayah was cooking. I walked into the kitchen and just stood there, admiring my girl for a moment. I bit my lip looking at her. She looked amazing from the back with her small waist and perfectly round ass. She didn't have on anything but one of my t-shirts and some panties. I was mesmerized.

"Take a picture, it lasts longer," she teased, and I laughed.

"You just look so good; I couldn't help but stare."

"You laying it on real thick this morning," she said smiling.

"Naw I laid it on you real thick last night," I said grabbing my dick.

"Ha ha, you're so hilarious. Come eat," I walked over to the island and looked to see what all she'd prepared. I had to admit, she showed out. She cooked scrambled eggs, grits, pancakes and bacon. I don't know who was about to eat this big ass breakfast, but I was going to try to eat as much as I could. Talayah fixed me a plate and then fixed herself a plate. We sat down at the island together and ate in silence for a few moments before I sparked up a conversation.

"What you got up today?" I asked.

"Nothing much, I gotta run into the shop and do a few heads but then I'm free. What are you doing today?" she asked. I was just about to answer her when my cell phone started vibrating on the kitchen counter. I got up to see who was calling me and smacked my lips when I saw who it was. I silenced the phone and sat back down.

"Who was that?" Talayah asked.

"Renae's ass," I said honestly. I didn't have to lie to her about shit. I noticed Talayah roll her eyes.

"What's wrong?" I questioned. She sighed and put her fork down before responding.

"Yasir, if we're going to be together, you gotta get that bitch in check. I don't have a problem checking her for you if I need to. I'll beat her ass again," she said sternly, and I smirked.

"Alright killa calm down," I joked. "I thought I made myself clear to her the night of my birthday but I see I haven't. I'll handle it. Don't worry," I said leaning over and pecking her lips.

"Yeah you better," she said getting up and putting her plate in the sink.

"I'm going to go ahead and get ready to go to the shop," she said and headed upstairs. I could tell she was still a little irritated by Renae's phone call, and one thing I didn't want was to piss her off or hurt her feelings at the very beginning of our relationship. Really, I never wanted to do those things, but I knew at some point it would be inevitable. I didn't want her to worry though, I'm going to handle Renae's ass and she's going to understand me loud and clear.

Talayah

I had to admit that I was on cloud fucking nine. Yasir's fine ass had finally snatched me up. It felt good to have a man treat you like a queen. He wasn't splurging on me or setting me up in a place, because I didn't need that. I could do all of that on my own. He spoiled me in ways that money can't buy. When I talked, he listened to understand and not to respond. When I cried, he lent me a shoulder and he's never passed judgement on me. I thought for sure after that day he found me laying on the ground, beat up and depressed that he would be completely turned off, but that day was the start of our bond. I really appreciated his friendship and now that we've taken it to the next level, I hope we never forgot what this was relationship was built on.

I quickly showered and headed to my shop before Yasir tried to hold me hostage and have me in the house fucking all day. I wouldn't mind it, but I had work to do and clients to service. I got to the shop in no time and it was packed. If I didn't have a reserved parking spot, I wouldn't be able to find parking. I smiled to myself. I'd really come a long way, but I still had a long way to go.

"Wassup boss lady!" Kree said standing at the front desk. I spoke to her and the rest of the girls as I made my way to my office. I caught up on some paperwork until Kree told me that my first client was here. I told her to go ahead and send my client to me and I began to set up.

"I'm so happy to be able to book with you. My boyfriend told me you were an amazing stylist," I heard a voice say from behind me. I turned around and when I realized who was sitting in my chair, I felt myself getting hot.

"What the fuck are you doing here?" I asked her. She gave me a look as if she had no clue what I was talking about.

"I'm here to get my hair done. Why else?" she asked, smirking. I chuckled and shook my head. I went to my office and grabbed my wallet then returned to the floor. I pulled out twenty-five dollars and handed it to her.

"Why are you giving me this?"

"That's your deposit. I'm returning it to you. I'm not going to be able to service you," I said trying to remain as professional as I possibly could.

"Yes, you are," she said handing me the money back. I wouldn't take it, so she got up and placed the money on my station behind me. I took that time to observe her appearance. I had to admit, shorty was beautiful, but she was a crazy ass bitch that I wanted out of my presence as soon as possible. I was ready to jump out of character, but I couldn't do that with customers and employees around.

"I came all this way for a service and I'm not leaving here without it," she said to me folding her arms and slightly rolling her neck. It took everything in me not to slap the shit out of her.

"Well I'll have one of my other stylists take care of you. You can go back out to the waiting area and wait for one of them to become available," I told her. There was no way in hell I would be the one to service her. She looked like she wanted to protest, but she didn't say anything else. She got up from my chair and stormed to the waiting area.

"Who the hell is that?" London asked. She was in the chair next to mine. I rolled my eyes.

"That's Yasir's girlfriend, ex, whatever. I really don't know what to call her," I said shrugging.

"Aww hell naw, what the hell is she in here for?"

"To start some shit and I'm not gonna give her the satisfaction," I told her.

"I know that's right," London said focusing her attention back on her client. I stood there for a while contemplating on what I should do about Renae's ass in the lobby. I was going to have one of the girl's service her for the sake of my business, but now that they knew who she was, no one would be willing to squeeze her in. Instead, I decided to just let her sit out there until she finally gave up and left. I would deal with any backlash from social media when it came.

I went on about my day and finished another client before I remembered that I left Renae sitting out in the waiting room. I hadn't heard anything from her, so I assumed she left. When I looked in the waiting room, it was empty and I silently thanked God.

I walked back to my station to clean up after my last client but was interrupted by the sound of Kree hollering.

"Boss lady!" Kree yelled from the front.

"Wassup?" I yelled back.

"Somebody's here to see you," she said walking over to me with a scared look on her face.

"Why you look like that? What's wrong? Who's here now?" I asked firing off question after question.

"The devil," she said to me and I gave her a confused look. That expression went away once I laid eyes on Antonio. I hadn't seen or heard from him since the day I walked out and seeing him now made me feel some type of way.

"What are you doing here?" I asked. The last time I saw him was at *Ruth Chris* and before that I hadn't seen him since he left my ass for dead.

"Can I talk to you?" he asked, and I looked at him like he was crazy.

"Talk to me about what? I don't think we have shit to talk about," I told him folding my arms under my breasts.

"Please just hear me out Lay," he begged. I looked at a man that I loved for damn near half my life. It was almost hard to believe that we'd gone from being lovers to me basically hating his guts. Every time I looked in his eyes I wanted to cry. He was a reminder of the darkest times and some of the happiest times of my life and I'd be lying if I say it didn't hurt to know that he didn't care enough about me to do right.

"Fine," I said reluctantly. I told my client that I'd be right back and led him to my office. Once we were both inside, I closed the door. I stood at the door with my arms folded waiting on him to say something, but several minutes passed and he still hadn't uttered a word.

"Are you going to talk or just stand there and look at me like I'm crazy?"

"I don't really know where to start Lay. You look good," he said, and I rolled my eyes.

"I know that," I told him, and he chuckled.

"You still mean as hell I see."

"What do you want Antonio? Get to the point," I said getting irritated with him.

"Ok. Ok. I really just want to apologize to you for the way our relationship ended. You didn't deserve that. I was drunk and I was trippin," he said, and I nodded my head.

"You were doing more than that. Is that all?" I said not caring to hear this same weak ass apology that he came with time after time.

"So, you got yourself a new man?" he asked, and I was a bit taken aback.

"What?" I asked with a frown on my face.

"I'm just sayin, I saw you at *Ruth Chris* the other day with some weak ass nigga. You really moved on?" he asked, and I sucked my teeth.

"So that's why you're really here. You think I finally moved on and found somebody else so you think you can just come in here with a sorry ass apology and get me back. That's what this is isn't it?"

"Nah, it ain't even like that. I just wanted to ask you, but I didn't know..." he started but I cut him off.

"You didn't know what?"

"I just didn't know how to come at you with it since..."

"Since the day you beat my ass and walked out, leaving me for dead," I reminded him.

"Lay, I ain't leave you for dead," he said.

"Yes you did! You stomped on me and beat me like I was a nigga on the street and walked the fuck out like I never meant shit to you! Do you understand that?! And you come in here asking me about some new nigga. Boy fuck you!" I yelled and he gave me a blank stare.

"Are you done?" he asked. "You poppin off all at the mouth but you still ain't answering my fucking question," he stated, and I could tell that he was getting agitated, but I didn't care. If he tried to do anything to me, I knew my girls were right outside and they'd ride for me no matter what.

"Yes, I got a new man and he's ten times the man that you could ever be. Does that make you feel better?" I asked and he nodded.

"Nah, it doesn't make me feel good, it actually makes me feel worse. Why would you go off and give another nigga my pussy like I wasn't coming back for that shit, huh? You my woman and you always gon be my woman until I say you aren't. Fuck wrong with you," he said, and I laughed.

"You gotta be delusional," I told him. This fool had really lost his mind. Before I could react, he lunged at me wrapping his hands around my neck. I quickly felt the oxygen leaving my lungs. My eyes grew wide and tears welled up.

"That nigga got you acting tough, huh? Do you really want to play with me Talayah?" he said through clenched teeth. The look in his eyes had me terrified. I'd only seen that look one other time and that was when he whooped my ass and walked out of my apartment that day.

"Please..." I managed to get out, barely above a whisper. I tried to claw at his hands, but it was no use. He had a pretty tight grip around my neck. Just as I felt my eyes rolling to the back of my head, my office door opened.

"Get your mothafuckin hands off of her!" I heard Giselle yell. "You bitch ass nigga!" A few seconds later, he released his grip and I slid down on the floor, coughing, and gasping for air. I looked up at Antonio who looked at me as if he was ready to end my life right there in my office and then I looked at Giselle who looked pissed the fuck off.

"I'll be seeing you again Lay Lay," he said with an evil glare on his face. In an instant, his face softened. He tried to walk over to me, but Giselle quickly stepped in front of him.

"I wish the fuck you would nigga," she said. Antonio smirked at her and then looked over to me, blowing me a kiss before walking out of the office. Once he was gone, Giselle turned to me.

"Are you okay?" she asked extending her hand to help me off of the floor. I didn't respond, I just broke down crying. She hugged me tight and patted my back.

"It's going to be okay best friend, I promise you. I tried to let you handle it your way, but now we're going to handle it my way," she said releasing me from her embrace and digging in her purse. She pulled out her iPhone and dialed a number. I didn't even have to ask her who she was calling, I already knew.

"Boss Lady, are you ok?" Kree asked handing me a bottle of water. I nodded my head, taking the bottle of water from her. "Something told me not to let his ass come back here with you, but I was just going to let you do your thing," she said.

"It's okay Kree. You couldn't have known he would act like that. Shit, I didn't know, but I should have," I said putting my head down. I was embarrassed to say the least. I always wanted my team to see me as this no nonsense boss bitch that had her shit together, but now I felt weak and stupid.

"Don't feel bad boss lady. We all got an Antonio in our lives. It happens. Just make sure you get a restraining order on that crazy mothafucka before he really hurts you," she said and then walked out of the office.

'Where the fuck he at?" Beanie said storming in the office.

"Nigga, did you fly here? I literally just texted you," Giselle told him.

"Now is not the time for you to be playing Giselle. Where that fuck nigga at?" he asked mugging her.

"He left. I walked in on him choking the shit out of her," she explained.

"I'm okay Beanie," I said, and he looked at me like I was crazy.

"No the fuck you ain't! You tryna protect this nigga?" he asked and I quickly shook my head no.

"Of course not! I just don't want you to get in the middle. I'll handle Antonio on my own," I told him taking a seat at my desk.

"How you gon do that Lay? You need to just let me and Yasir handle it,".

"Hell no! Yasir and I literally just started our relationship. I don't want to make my problems his problems," I told them.

"When the hell did that happen?" Giselle asked.

"Last night," I said unable to control the smile that spread across my face.

"Bitch you finally gave him some!" Giselle squealed. I glanced at Beanie who had his nose turned up like he was disgusted.

"Man, I don't wanna hear that shit! I'll be in the lobby. I'm not leaving until you are Talayah, and from here on out I'm gonna have one of my guys here at all times to protect y'all. This shit ain't gon happen again," he said. I opened my mouth to speak but he cut me off. "I don't wanna hear shit you got to say about it. You got to let me protect you some kind of way," Beanie said, and I smiled.

"Okay, but can you make it so that Yasir doesn't know. I don't want to drag him into this This isn't his issue," I told him.

"Lay if that's your man then he needs to know. He'd want to protect you just as much as me," he said.

"Yeah, but I can't risk him getting hurt over my bullshit with Antonio. I'm agreeing to having one of your guys tail me for a while to make sure I'm good, but Yasir knows nothing about this. Understood?" I asked and Beanie nodded his head.

"Thanks bro," I told him, and he walked out of the office. Giselle closed the door behind him and then took a seat in one of the chairs across from my desk.

"Bitch! Before we start talking about Yasir, I need to tell you something," she said to me.

"Ok, what?"

"You know I love you like my Mama pushed you out herself, so I'm not going to sugar coat shit," she started. "You need to get a restraining order and you need to get a gun. I don't know why you're protecting this nigga and won't let Beanie handle him for you, but you can't be defenseless. I'm going to have Beanie change your locks and I'm getting you some mace. If I gotta drag you down to the courthouse to get this restraining order then that's just what we'll do. I'll drag yo ass to the CCW class too," she said, and I just stared at her.

"I don't think I need to shoot him to get him to leave me alone," I said, and Giselle sucked her teeth.

"Did he choke the sense out of you? What part of crazy do you not understand? This is just the beginning. Next he'll be popping up at your house or random places trying to make it seem like a coincidence. He will seriously hurt you, or worse kill you. I'm not trying to bury you Talayah," she said with tears in her eyes. One thing about Giselle, she wasn't a cry baby. Crying was always my thing.

"Don't cry G," I said grabbing her hand. "I'll handle him, I promise."

Antonio

That bitch wanted to act like she was all high and mighty but I knew how to bring her ass back to reality. She had me fucked up if she thought I was just going to let her be happy with whatever nigga she called herself fucking with right now. She belonged to me and I wanted her back. She could come willingly, or I'd force her to. That would be up to her.

As I was getting into my car, I noticed that one of the females who had just came out of the shop a few hours ago was coming out of the boutique next door. Shorty was bad as hell too. She was dressed casually in some jeans and a t-shirt, with her hair pulled up into a bun and some lip gloss on her lips. Immediately I imagined how her lips would feel wrapped around my dick.

"Can I talk to you for a minute?" I called out. She stopped walking and started looking around trying to figure out where my voice had just come from. When our eyes connected, I smirked and walked over to her.

"How are you beautiful?" I asked and she smiled shyly.

"I'm fine. How are you?" she asked.

"Better now. I know you don't know me from a can of paint, but I was wondering if we could get to know each other. Go out to eat, movies, something like that?" I asked shooting my shot. I was going to engage in some small talk, but I figured it was better to get straight to the point.

"How do I know you ain't a serial killer or a psychopath?" she asked, and I chuckled.

"Shit, you don't, but I can tell you wanna find out," I said cockily, and she looked away nervously. She reached into her purse and pulled her cell phone out handing it to me. I grabbed it and plugged my number in. Shit was easier than I thought. She didn't ask me if I had a girl or none of that shit these other hoes ask.

"Make sure you use that," I told her. She said nothing, only nodded her head and walked away. I watched her ass giggle from left to right and felt myself getting hard. I quickly adjusted myself, headed to my car and pulled off.

I pulled up to my house, well, LaCorsha's house and sat in the car for a minute. I was trying to calm myself down before I stepped foot in that house. I was still kind of pissed about what happened with Talayah and I didn't need Co picking up on shit. I don't know what it is, but Co was like a shark and I was fresh meat when it came to how I was feeling. She could sense my energy was off from a mile away and I didn't need her nagging me about anything. After about ten minutes of sitting in the car, I got out and made my way to the front door. Using the key she gave me, I turned the locks and was met by LaCorsha standing in the foyer with a scowl on her face.

"Fuck wrong with you?" I asked.

"Why were you sitting out in the car for so long instead of just coming in?" she asked, her tone dripping with attitude. I took a deep breath and sighed. She was starting with the bullshit already.

"I was trying to calm down so I wouldn't take my anger out on you," I told her walking past her and heading to the kitchen.

"What's wrong baby?" she asked, her tone a little softer.

"Nothing, I've just had a long day and I just wanna chill," I told her, and she nodded. I grabbed a bottle of water, twisted the top off and drank from it. I looked at Co and admired her for a moment. She was almost five months pregnant and the growing baby bump made it obvious that she was pregnant. She was so small, so any little pudge was noticeable. She looked beautiful pregnant. I can see that pregnancy glow shit I heard people talking about Her hair was pulled up into a ponytail, and she was dressed down in a simple white shirt and black Nike shorts.

"Okay, we can do that," she said walking over to me and biting her bottom lip. She kneeled down in front of me and pulled my jogging pants down. Before she was able to pull my dick out, I stopped her.

"Nah, I want to actually chill," I told her, and I heard her smack her lips.

"Are you seriously turning me down right now?" she asked.

"I'm not turning you down, I'm just not in the mood."

"Since when are you not in the mood? You're a nigga, y'all are always in the mood," I rubbed my temples in an attempt to calm my nerves.

"You must be fucking somebody else. You would never give me that weak ass excuse," she said, and I lost it. I threw the water bottle at her, rushed over to her and grabbed her throat.

"Bitch I just told you I had a bad day and I want to relax! Leave me the fuck alone! I'll fuck you when I feel like it. Go sit yo ass down somewhere," I yelled flinging her to the floor. I looked at her laying on the ground crying and images of Talayah in that same position came to mind. Instantly, I felt like shit. I looked at her holding her stomach and crying.

"FUCK MAN!" I shouted punching the wall. "Are you ok?" I asked her.

"Get the hell away from me Antonio!" she screamed. I wanted to at least help her off the floor. I didn't want to make the same mistake twice and just leave her laying there, but I decided against it. I grabbed my keys off of the kitchen counter and walked out of the house. I couldn't stay in that house with her tonight, I was liable to kill her and the last thing I wanted to do was harm my seed.

I climbed in my car and sped off with no particular destination in mind. I didn't have anyone to turn to in this moment. Usually, when I was feeling like this it would be because of Talayah and I'd just go to LaCorsha, but I didn't have either one of them at the moment. I found myself pulling into Zino's. I walked in and immediately noticed that the bar was dead with the exception of a couple of old heads, the bartenders and a female sitting at the bar with her head down. I walked over to the bar and took a seat. Shortly after, the bartender came over, took my drink order and left me alone with my thoughts. I knew I was fucking up, but I couldn't help the way I was feeling. There was a rage building inside of me that I couldn't put out no matter how hard I tried. The bartender came over and placed my drink in front of me. I gulped it down, enjoying the burning sensation going down my throat and immediately ordered another one. Just as I was about to pull my phone out, I heard sniffles to the right of me. I looked over and noticed the girl with her head down was crying. I slightly rolled my eyes. I was so tired of seeing females cry. I almost wanted to choke this bitch to get her to shut the hell up.

"Aye, fuck is wrong with you?" I asked. I know my tone came across as rude, but I didn't care. She was lucky I didn't tell her to shut the fuck up. The girl looked over at me and I realized that she was the pretty bartender that I always tried to hit on when I was here. She looked at me, sucked her teeth and rolled her eyes.

"Don't say shit to me," she said.

"I wouldn't have but you over here loud as hell. I just want you to shut up," I told her, and she laughed. "That's funny?"

"Nah, but you funny. Who the fuck are you to come in here talking to somebody like you own the place," she said with a slight attitude.

"I could if I wanted to and I could buy yo hoe ass too," I responded. I thought she was about to cuss me out, slap me or something, but she did the opposite. She wiped her eyes and gave me a look that I couldn't really read.

"Is that right?" she asked in a seductive tone.

"You tryna find out?" I asked.

"Maybe I am," she said. I stood up, grabbed her arm and lightly pulled her to the back of the bar where the restrooms were. Once in the men's restroom, I locked the door and pushed her up against it. I didn't waste time tugging at her jeans to get them off. She leaned in to kiss me, but I wasn't feeling that. I moved my head and she started sucking on my neck. I wasn't feeling that either, so I grabbed her by her throat. I guess you could say I had a thing for choking bitches. I expected her to be afraid, but instead, she smiled.

"Oh, you like it rough I see," I stated, and she nodded her

head yes. I smirked and let go of her neck long enough to snatch her jeans down and rip her panties off.

"Go in the stall," I instructed, and she did as she was told. "Now bend over."

She immediately bent over the toilet, placing her bare hands on the toilet seat. I stroked my dick looking at the sight of her caramel ass in the air and slowly entered her. She was wet, but not wet enough. I reached in front of her and started playing with her clit to get her wetter, but she wouldn't.

"Man, fuck this!" I stated pulling out of her and pulling my boxers and pants up.

"What's wrong?" she asked standing up straight.

"Bitch you ain't even wet! How I'm supposed to get in that dry ass shit? I've been fantasizing about your ass since I started coming in this bitch and this is what I get?" I yelled, disgusted. She looked embarrassed, but I didn't care. I unlocked the bathroom stall and stormed out of the bar. I got into my car and sped off with no destination in mind. All I wanted to do was relieve some stress and every bitch I came in contact with was on some other shit. I was doing about fifty miles-per-hour down a residential street, but I didn't give a fuck. I felt so alone, like I had nobody. I didn't have any siblings to turn to, no parents, no grandparents, nobody. The one person that I could count on, I shitted on. I needed her back. I had to find a way to make it right with her. I quickly pat my pockets for my phone but couldn't feel it. I reached over to the passenger side seat to feel for my phone, but I still couldn't get my hand on it. I looked at the seat for a second to try to look for it and out of nowhere I heard a horn blaring. I viciously turned the wheel not knowing where the other car was coming from.

SKRRRRRTTT!!! BOOM!!!! The sound of glass shattering and tires screeching was all I heard before everything went black.

Yasir

"Where you at?" I asked Renae. She'd been blowing my phone up every day and Talayah was fed up with it, so I wanted to go ahead and nip this shit in the bud now.

"Home," she said.

"I'll be there in fifteen minutes," I told her and hung up.

"Where you going?" Talayah asked entering the kitchen. I smiled looking at my baby. I told her ass that we needed each other that day at her shop and I knew I wasn't wrong. The way this girl made me feel was something that I've never experienced and I liked it. I hope that I've been making her just as happy, and I would continue to do so for as long as she let me.

"I'm about to go handle this issue with Renae," I said honestly.

"Handle it how?" she asked with a skeptical expression on her face.

"Not sexually and not violently if that's what you mean," I chuckled, and she shrugged.

"Just checking," she said putting her hands up in mock surrender. "When will you be back?"

"A couple of hours. After I leave her spot I'm going to check on some things at the office. Make sure everything is as it should be."

"Oh, how did it go with that employee you were telling me about?" she asked, and I smiled. I loved that she actually listened to me and seemed to genuinely give a fuck about the shit that I had going on.

"Good. I promoted him. Which reminds me, I told him that I would take him and his girl to dinner to celebrate and I need you by my side," I stated, and she nodded.

"Of course. When?" she asked.

"Friday," I told her, and she agreed. I kissed her, grabbed my phone and keys and then left out of the house.

I made it to Renae's house and parked in the driveway. Her car wasn't outside but I figured it was in the garage. I walked up to the front door and knocked. A few seconds later she answered the door in a pair of shorts and a tank top.

"So I gotta blow your phone up for you to come see me?" she asked seductively.

"I'm not here for all of that," I said ready to get away from her.

"Well what are you here for?" she asked.

"Yo ass gotta stop blowing my phone up like that Renae. I told you the night of my birthday you ain't my girl and I'm done fucking with you like that. I apologize if I ever led you on or made you feel like we were something that we weren't," I said repeating myself. "But you need to chill the fuck out. You making my girl uncomfortable and I don't like that shit," I told her. I looked in her eyes and it seemed like all the color drained from her flawless skin.

"Your...girl?" she asked sounding like she was on the verge of tears.

"That's what I said," I told her. "Look, I don't have a lot of time to stand here and talk to you, it's really very simple. Whatever we had is done. It was fun, but I found somebody that I really fuck with and I'm not trying to lose her. I know there's a man out there that will love you the way you want to be loved, but that man ain't me," I said and turned to walk away. I walked about three or four steps before I felt her punch me in the back of my head.

"You ain't shit! I've been by your side for the longest and you just leave me high and dry for some new bitch you just met!? Are you serious!? I hate you!!" she screamed raining blow after blow on my back. I was taught to never beat on a woman, but she was about to make me forget about all my home training. I quickly spun around and caught her wrist.

"KEEP YO MOTHAFUCKIN HANDS OFF OF ME!" I yelled

pushing her to the ground.

"Fuck you!" she yelled, now crying.

"Nah, you ain't never getting the chance to fuck me again," I said calmly, speed walking to my car. I got inside, let out a deep breath and pulled off. I really hope she wasn't going to become a bigger problem. I was taught that you never harm the kids and the women but if she kept on, I wouldn't hesitate to silence her forever.

I drove in the direction of 3M hoping that everything was running smoothly there. I really didn't want to deal with no more bullshit today. I made it to 3M in about twenty minutes and headed straight up to my office. I'd been there for about thirty minutes completing paperwork before I decided to check on my lines. As I was walking up and down the lines I noticed that Antonio wasn't there. I wanted to talk to him about his promotion and have him fill out some paperwork. I grabbed one of the other supervisors and pulled them to the side.

"Hey, where is James?" I asked.

"He got into an accident and is in the hospital, but they said it wasn't severe so he should be back in the next week or so."

"Oh ok, I'm glad it wasn't severe. Everything else good?" I asked and he nodded. I took that as my queue to go ahead and head home. I wanted to take Talayah out and show her a good time.

I made it home in no time and when I entered the house, it was silent, like no one was here.

"Lay," I called out, but she didn't answer. I looked in every room on the first floor and even went in the basement, but she wasn't there. I made my way up the stairs and entered the bedroom, but she wasn't in there either. I was just about to call her name again when I heard sniffling coming from the bathroom. I walked over to the door and knocked.

"Lay, you ok?" I asked. I heard more sniffing before I opened the door and found her on the bathroom floor with her knees to her chest, crying.

"What's wrong bae?" I asked sitting down beside her.

"Nothing, I'm ok. I'm sorry," she said wiping her face.

"No, you in here crying, so what's wrong? Talk to me," I told her, concerned. When I left the house this morning she was just fine.

"My ex-boyfriend is in the hospital," she said sniffing again. I felt myself getting angry, but I had to remember that she'd been with this man for years and feelings just don't go away.

"Damn, what happened?" I asked.

"I'm not really sure. I just know he's in the hospital. I don't know how he's doing or anything," she said.

"Well, do you want to go see him? Do you know what hospital he's in?"

"I know what hospital he's in, but I don't know if I should go see him," she stated.

"Why?"

"I don't want to disrespect or upset you," she said, and I hugged her and kissed the top of her head.

"I know that you care about the nigga, so I'm not going to be upset if you want to go check and see how he's doing. I'll even go with you," I offered, and she looked at me with teary eyes.

"You'd do that even after knowing how he's treated me?"

"Yeah, of course. I mean, I ain't gon' go in the nigga room or nothing like that, but I'll take you and wait in the lobby," I said.

"No, that's ok. I think I'm just going to take Giselle with me," she said, and I nodded my head. She got herself together and then exited the bathroom. As much as I tried to act like it wasn't bothering me, I was annoyed that she wanted to go check on his bitch ass after he basically left her for dead, but I wasn't going to stress her out or make her feel small for feeling the way she did. I just hoped he didn't try to make her feel guilty and she end up back with him. If that happened, it was bound to be a problem.

Talayah

My emotions were all over the place as I pulled into the hospital parking lot. I told Yasir that Giselle was coming with me, but I lied. I just didn't want him to come with me. It felt weird having my new boyfriend with me to go check on my old one. I felt weird even being here, but my other half felt like I at least had to go make sure he was alive. I sat in the car staring at the hospital entrance for what seemed like forever. Finally, I turned the engine off, got out and made my way to the entrance.

Once I made it inside, I asked the lady at the front desk for Antonio's room number. The ride up to his floor was making my nerves even worse. I felt like I was going to meet with the devil, and I contemplated on pressing the button to go back down to the lobby. Just as I was about to press the button, the doors opened. I walked onto the fourth floor and followed the directions the lady had given me earlier. Once I made it to his room, I took a deep breath before entering and when I did, he was sleeping. He looked so at peace, almost like he was dead. The only reason that I knew he was still alive was because of the beeping of the monitor they had him hooked up to. I grabbed the chair by his bed and scooted it up to his bedside before taking a seat. The screeching sound of the chair scooting up must have woke him up because his eyes opened. He took a minute to wake up and when he noticed I was sitting beside him, he smiled.

"I knew you would come see me. I knew you still loved me," he said.

"I wouldn't say all of that," I told him, and he frowned.

"You don't love me? I can't tell. You came up here to check on me, that's gotta mean something," he said.

"Antonio, I just wanted to make sure you were ok. I'm not in love with you anymore but that doesn't mean I don't give a fuck if you live or die," I said getting up from the chair.

"Where are you going?" he asked.

"I just said I came to see if you were alive. You're alive, so now I'm leaving," I said making my way towards the door.

"Lay Lay, please don't leave. I'm sorry. Can you please just sit and talk with me. I miss you," he pleaded. The tone of his voice tugged at my heart strings and it pissed me off. I wasn't supposed to come here for old feelings. I was only supposed to say my peace and be done. Against my better judgement, I sat back down.

"Antonio, let me just say what I need to say and then I'm leaving," I said in a stern tone and he nodded his head. "Do I love you? Yes. There will always be a piece of me that will care about you," I stated, and I saw a smile start to appear on his face. "But," I continued and instantly the smile left his face.

"You did me so wrong. We were together for years, and no it wasn't all bad, but as soon as it started to get hard for you, you started showing your true colors. Yeah, you cheated before and you could be an asshole, but I knew you actually gave a fuck. Then, somewhere along the line you just stopped caring. The deeper into depression you fell, the more you started to take it out on me. You verbally, physically, mentally and emotionally abused me. You found a way to make me feel as if I was less than, like it didn't matter whether I was alive or dead. Antonio, you beat me so bad that day you walked out that I contemplated ending my life. I can never forgive you for that. I found somebody that cares. He makes me feel safe and make me want to be a better woman and I can't put all my trust and faith in to him because of all the damage you did. But no more. I refuse to let you continue to have control over me anymore. You don't deserve it. So, I hope that you get well soon, and I wish you the best, but I'm done," I said standing up again.

I started towards the door, but he called my name again. I looked back at the man that I used to love, and my heart broke for the very last time. I felt the tears forming in my eyes but I refused to let them fall.

"I'm sorry," he said, and I nodded my head.

"Yeah, you are," I responded and left out of the room. I rushed back to my car and cried my eyes out. I vowed to myself that this was the last time that I'd ever allow tears to fall out of my eyes because of Antonio. I was taking my power back.

Once I was done, I drove back to Yasir's house and knocked. A few moments later he opened the door wearing nothing but some gray jogging pants. He looked at me and stepped to the side to let me in.

"You ok?" he asked, and I nodded. "You sure?"

"Yeah, I really just want you to hold me," I told him, and he nodded. We went upstairs to the bedroom, I took a quick shower and then got into the bed. Yasir was already laying down waiting on me. I curled up on his chest and enjoyed the feeling of being in his arms. I felt so protected, like nothing could ever hurt me when he was around. It was a feeling that was new to me, but something that I could get used to. I felt Yasir kiss the top of my head and I smiled. It was at that moment that I knew I didn't want to be anywhere else.

Antonio

I was finally getting out of the hospital and in a few days, I'd be going back to work. I thought the day that Talayah came to see me she would come saying she wanted to make us work, but it was the exact opposite. The look in her eye was something that I'd never seen before, and I didn't like that shit one bit. I even told her I was sorry, and she still wouldn't change her mind. I was going to have to figure out another way to get her back. I wanted her to come back willingly, but I'd force her if I had to.

LaCorsha walked in the room, smiling and I rolled my eyes. She had been happy as hell lately too and I know it wasn't because of me.

"Fuck is up Co?" I asked.

"What do you mean?"

"Why yo ass walking around so happy?" I questioned and she laughed.

"Are you serious? I can't be happy?"

"Well I know it ain't because of me. I haven't been around to give you no dick so what the fuck got you so happy?"

"Wow. You're serious. If you must know, I'm just happy that you're getting out," she said walking over to me and grabbing my crotch. "I would love some of that too, but I can wait," she said.

"Yeah, alright, let me find out another nigga been inside you while you're carrying my seed. I'mma send you and it to the fuckin' morgue," I told her seriously.

"Okay crazy," she said laughing, but I was dead ass serious. We waited around for the doctor to discharge me and then we left. Co drove us back to her house, well, I guess our house now, and I couldn't wait to get some time to think and put my plan in motion. We were getting settled when Co told me that she was going to the grocery store to pick up some things she needed for dinner tonight. I was happy for the time alone, because I needed to come up with a plan to get my girl back. I was still in shock that we were actually done even though I was the one who left. I just always thought she would feel like she was stuck. This new found inner strength she possesses has to be coming from whatever nigga she was fucking. I knew at some point I would have to get him out the way if I wanted to get Talayah back. Then, not only was that nigga an issue, but I had a whole kid on the way that I knew she wasn't going to willingly accept. I had to be strategic about all of this, because I couldn't lose both of my bitches, one of them had to stay around. I had feelings for both, but I'd take Talayah over Co any day, anytime.

• •

A few days passed and I was ready to get back to work. I hoped that I still had my promotion and I was going to make sure I talked to Mr. White once I got there. That bonus that came with the position was very well needed. It would put me in the position to make sure my kid, baby mom, and I were straight forever.

"You look good Mr. Manager," LaCorsha said hugging me from behind.

"Thanks," I said adjusting my tie.

"I hope you have a great first day," she said.

"What are you going to be doing?" I asked her.

"Just working. I'mma just work from home while I'm pregnant," she said, and I nodded my head. LaCorsha worked as an advertising promotions and marketing manager. She was the boss at her marketing firm so she can choose not to be there whenever she wants. I said my goodbyes and left out for work. Once there, I headed straight to Mr. White's office without letting his secretary know. I knocked before I entered the office.

"Mr. James, how are you feeling?" he asked.

"A lot better, ready to work. I hope the position still stands," I said getting straight to the point.

"Of course. I always stay true to my word. Let me show you

to your office," he said, and I followed him. I was finally a salaried employee instead of hourly. The office that he gave me was nice as fuck. Unlike anything I've ever had before. Everything was finally falling into place, except my love life. My dumb ass was starting a family with a girl I wasn't even in love with, and I can't get that shit out of my head. I needed Talayah back in my life, but I didn't need all that bullshit that came with her. The nagging, the arguing, that shit was for the birds. I was so fucking confused.

"Are we still on for dinner? I know since the accident you've been out of commission, but congratulations are still in order," he said breaking me out of my thoughts.

"Yeah, of course. When?" I asked.

"I'm thinking next Friday or Saturday. I want you to be able to settle in your new position," he said, and I nodded.

"That's fine with me. Next Friday will be fine."

"Alright, cool. I'll catch up with you," he said walking out of the office. I finished up the rest of the day pretty quickly and went home. I wanted to take LaCorsha out to celebrate. She's been bitching that we haven't really been able to spend any real time together since the accident, so I was going to take her out to shut her up.

"Co!" I yelled.

"In the kitchen," she said.

"Bro, yo fat ass eating again?" I joked. I walked in the kitchen to find Co mugging me. "What?" I asked confused.

"You really just called me fat like I'm not pregnant with your whole baby," she said, and I rubbed my hand down my face.

"I ain't mean it like that bae. I was just joking," I said smiling trying to lighten the mood.

"That ain't funny Antonio," she said folding her arms.

"Man cut it out. I said I was sorry. I came home tryna take you out, not to argue," I told her and then her face lit up.

"Really?" she said in a child-like tone.

"Yes, really, so hurry up and come on," I said, and she hurried out of the kitchen. I laughed and shook my head. They say food is the way to a man's heart, but in LaCorsha's case it's definitely the other way around.

Yasir

I was currently on my way home from work, but I kind of didn't want to go home yet. Talayah went back to her house after that day she visited her ex in the hospital, and ever since then her attitude has shifted. When I asked her what was going on, she told me she was fine, but I could see right through it. I didn't want to pressure her or anything, so I was just giving her the space I think she needed. I'd been lonely as fuck this past week and I really missed her. Instead of going home, I made a U-Turn and headed to Talayah's house. It took me no time to get to her house and once I arrived, I ran up to her door and banged on it like I was the police.

Talayah opened the door looking good as fuck in a pair of shorts and a tank top. Her hair was in a bun on the top of her head. She was just chilling around the crib, no make-up or nothing, but her skin was glowing. She was beautiful to me, inside and out.

"Wassup baby?" I asked hugging her.

"What are you doing here?" she asked, hugging me back and then kissing me on my lips.

"I just wanted to come and see you. I miss you. I haven't really seen you this past week, so I just wanted to see your face," I told her, and she smiled.

"I miss you too baby. I'm sorry I've been so distant, I've just been..." she started to say but I cut her off.

"You ain't gotta explain it to me. I get it," I told her. I really didn't want to hear nothing coming out of her mouth about her ex, even though I know she felt some type of way.

"Thank you," she said kissing me again. "You wanna come in?" she asked, and I nodded.

"Oh, my bad Giselle, I ain't know you were here," I said. "I ain't mean to interrupt y'all girl time," I said air quoting girl's time and laughing.

"Whatever. I was about to leave anyway. Go ahead and dick her down," she said, and I laughed.

"Trust me, I will," I told her smirking at Talayah.

"You nasty," Talayah said wrapping her arms around me. Giselle left and we were left alone.

"I really did miss you," I said kissing her.

"I missed you too baby," she said slipping her tongue in my mouth. I responded by grabbing her ass and she moaned softly. I took that as my queue to lead her back to her bedroom.

Antonia

Today was the day that I was officially being promoted. I mean, it was official on paper, but it wasn't official to me until I had this dinner with Mr. White. Nobody in the company, or at least my department had ever been extended an offer to break bread with him and discuss business. I felt like that really meant I was something special. I had something that no other employee on that line had. He knew that one day I could run this company with my eyes closed and I planned on doing just that. I saw our relationship going beyond business. I had to surround myself with the type of men that I wanted to be in order to reach higher.

"Which tie?" I asked Co. We've been ok lately. Of course, she was still getting on my fucking nerves, but I was blaming it on the pregnancy. Plus, I wasn't trying to piss her off. At least not until I had Talayah back, then I would decide which one I wanted.

"The black one. Can't go wrong with black or blue," she said, and I agreed. I chose to go the simple route with a dark blue button up, black tie and black slacks. I gave the black tie to LaCorsha and had her put it on for me. Looking at her, I admired her frame. She was starting to show since she was now almost four months pregnant. She had on a navy off the shoulder dress that came down to her knees and some clear heels. She had just gotten her hair done in a high ponytail that came down to the middle of her back. She looked good.

"You look good," I said kissing her. She smiled and kissed me again.

"Thank you, baby, you don't look too bad yourself," We left out of the house and rode to the restaurant in a comfortable silence. I felt good about what was going to come from this dinner. It was the first of many and the start to me making some real money.

Talayah

I felt bad about distancing myself from Yasir and I was happy as hell that he just showed up at my doorstep. He fucked my brains out. He never wanted me to go through shit by myself, which is what I liked about him. He was the total opposite of Antonio, and I swear I felt like I was on cloud nine when he was around. He made me feel safe and secure, and I'd never felt that feeling before. I kind of felt like it was all happening so fast, but I couldn't stop the way that I'm feeling. I think I was falling in love with this man, and I hoped I wasn't in this alone. I wasn't going to say a word until he did though.

"Babe!" Yasir yelled snapping me out of my thoughts. I slightly jumped and he frowned. "Are you ok?" he asked.

"Yeah, I'm good, you just scared me, that's all."

"Alright. What you got up for today?"

"I'm going up to the shop. I don't have any clients but I'm going to take some walk ins. I haven't really been working lately, I need to get back in my bag, especially if I want to open up a second location," I told him, and he smiled.

"A second location? That's dope. I can help you with that if you need me to," he offered. That right there is exactly what I'm talking about. The man was a freaking God-send.

"I'm good for now baby, but I'll let you know. I'm sure I'll need your help at some point though," I said getting off the bed and kissing him. He stuck his tongue in my mouth and our tongues intertwined. He grabbed my ass and I slightly moaned but he pulled away.

"Girl you tryna get something started and we both need to get to work. Get on before I fuck the shit out of you," he said slapping my ass.

"What if I want you to?" I asked seductively.

"I got you tonight fasho. We got money to be made today though. Now get to work freaky ass," he said kissing me on my lips and walking out of the bedroom.

"You do know I own the shop and I can go in when I want to right?" I yelled and I heard him laugh. Begrudgingly, I got up to take care of my hygiene and get myself ready for the day. Once I was out of the shower, I went into my closet to find something to wear for the day. I decided to settle on comfortable, but cute. I laid out a neon Nike sweatshirt, some black Nike leggings and black and neon Nike air maxes. I pulled my hair into a high ponytail and applied some lashes and lip gloss. I didn't feel like doing too much today, but I still wanted to be cute. I raced down the stairs and was about to whip up some breakfast for Yasir and I. Once I got to the kitchen, I heard him talking on the phone.

"I'm sick of dealing with this bitch B, we gotta find a way to get her off my fucking back," he said, piquing my interest. "I never thought fucking with her would bring me this much drama and headache. I need her gone," he continued and then paused. "Alright, bet," he said and then hung up the phone. I made my presence known by standing in the doorway with my arms folded. I wondered who he was talking about. I had a feeling about who it was, but I wasn't going to ask him. I wanted him to be able to come to me.

"You good?" I asked and he rushed to put his phone in his pocket.

"Yeah, I'm good. Are you still coming with me to that dinner tonight? I want you to meet my new supervisor I've been talking to you about," he said, and I nodded.

"The one that you said don't take no shit?" I asked and he nodded. "Yeah, I can't wait to meet him. Sounds like my kind of dude," I said, and he frowned.

"Yeah whatever don't be flirting with the nigga or his pregnant girlfriend gon beat yo ass," he joked.

"Whatever, sis don't want no smoke," I said grabbing my purse and keys.

"Damn, no breakfast?" he asked.

"Nope, I don't feel like making breakfast for ya big head ass no more," I said sticking my tongue out at him and heading out the door to my car.

"You wrong as fuck," he said coming behind me. We said our goodbyes and then I headed to the shop. It felt like I hadn't seen my girls in months. I pulled up to Black Girl Magic, parked in my usual spot and got out. Walking into the shop, I felt at home. I went to my office and found Giselle sitting there.

"Bitch what are you doing here? Don't you have some news to report or some shit," I joked, and she threw the middle finger up at me.

"Bitch I made an appointment with you a long ass time ago. Yo trifling ass forgot," she said, and I put my hand to my mouth.

"Damn, I definitely forgot. Well, I ain't got no appointments or nothing today, so come on," I told her. I fixed Giselle's hair and caught up with the girls a little bit. It felt good just kicking it in the shop. Giselle and I decided to grab some lunch, but before I could make it back to my office to grab my purse, somebody busted through the shop door.

"Where the fuck is Talayah?" I turned around and found the same bitch that we fought at the club that day. I rolled my eyes. I really didn't feel like dealing with none of this bullshit.

"What the fuck are you doing here?" I asked.

"I came to talk to you, woman to woman," she said.

"Hell naw, not woman to woman. What, you still fucking Yasir?" Giselle asked.

"If I am it ain't none of your mothafuckin business and I ain't talking to your bum ass anyway," she stated. Giselle started to charge at her, but I pulled her back.

"Ain't gon be none of that shit in my shop. You got something to say just say it now," I told her. I was ready for her to get the fuck out of my place of business and I didn't want Giselle beating her ass...again.

"I'm pregnant," she said, and I swear it felt like the wind was knocked out of me.

"Say that again?" I asked looking at her. She smirked at me like she had the upper hand.

"I'm...pregnant," she replied. I started to open my mouth, but she cut me off. "Before you even say that dumb ass shit, yes, it's Yasir's. I wouldn't even be in this bitch claiming to be pregnant if it wasn't his," she said.

"What are you telling me for? Why aren't you telling Yasir?"

"Because the nigga blocked and threatened me, so I have no way of getting in touch with him," she said sounding desperate. I rolled my eyes.

"Well find another way and get the fuck out my shop. I'm not relaying messages for you and you don't put no fear in my heart, coming in here talking about you pregnant. That ain't gon change what me and him got going on," I told her, and she rolled her eyes. "Bitch, I said beat it," I told her, and she walked out of the shop. As soon as she left, I went to my office and broke down. Giselle was right behind me.

"It's okay best friend, I'm sure that bitch was just trying to get under your skin. Don't let her win. Just talk to your man," she said. I continued to cry for a few more minutes and then I got myself together.

"I'm definitely going to have a conversation with his ass. If she's pregnant they had to be fucking around this entire time, right?" I asked.

"You don't know that. You and Yasir have only been together for a couple of months Talayah."

"You're supposed to be on my side," I told her.

"I am, but I also want you to consider every possibility. I don't think Yasir has cheated on you. Has he ever given you a reason not to trust him?" she asked, and I shook my head no. "Exactly, so just go talk to him," she said. I looked at the clock and realized I had to make it home for this dinner with Yasir's new supervisor.

"You right G. I'm gonna talk to him later. I gotta head to his house anyway and get ready for this dinner," I told her and wiped my face.

"Bitch don't kill him," she said, and I chuckled.

"I'm not G. I'm not," I said hugging her. A few seconds later Kree knocked on the door.

"Boss lady you got a package out here," she said. I got up to sign for whatever the package was. Once I got to the lobby, I realized it was a beautiful bouquet of roses. A huge smile spread across my face. I looked at the flowers and realized there was a card. I grabbed the card and read it: *Just because.* I cheesed from ear to ear, admiring the beautiful bouquet. Yasir was so sweet to me. I hate that I even considered that he could have gotten that bitch pregnant. I knew better than that. He had never given me a reason to believe he was on some fuck shit, so I had no reason to act like he was. He wasn't Antonio.

Giselle left and shortly after I received my flowers and I left out right behind her. I made it to Yasir's house in no time, but I didn't go in immediately. I didn't know if I wanted to talk to him about what happened at the shop or just act like everything was okay. I wanted to be rational, but I wasn't sure how I was going to react when I actually saw his face. I decided to just go in the house and let the chips fall where they may.

I made it up to the bedroom and found Yasir putting on his watch in the mirror. I leaned against the doorway just staring at him. His milk chocolate complexion was buttery, smooth and sexy. He had on a burgundy button up, a black tie and black slacks. I guess I was staring too hard because Yasir cleared his throat.

"You see something you like?" he asked biting down on his lip.

"Hell yeah I do," I said walking up to him and wrapping my arms around his neck. I kissed him but pulled away before it got too intense. "Bae I gotta talk to you about something."

"What's wrong?" I proceeded to tell him about what happened at the shop earlier.

"Did you see a pregnancy test?" he asked.

"Naw, I didn't. She just screamed it from the mountain top," I told him.

"Man, she ain't pregnant. That bitch crazy as fuck. I haven't

136

slept with her since before I got with you and I didn't cum in her," he assured me, and I believed him.

"I believe you. You've never given me a reason not to trust you," I told him, and he smiled.

"That's right. Ride with ya man. I'm never gonna have you out here looking crazy, period," he said and kissed my lips.

"How long are we going to be at this dinner? I really don't wanna spend all night with your employee and some pregnant lady," I said, and he chuckled.

"Not long. We're just going to break bread together and dip. I need to really talk with him outside the workplace and pick his brain. I know he has some really good ideas for the company, and I want to hear him out, but he can't really express himself when he's at work because mothafuckas in that bitch be hatin'. I've witnessed that shit myself. But if he's got what it takes like I think he does he could eventually take my spot," he told me, and I nodded my head.

"I get it. Business comes first. I'm going to go ahead and get dressed," I said pulling away from him and heading to the bathroom. Before I got in the shower, I remembered the flowers that he gave me that were downstairs. "And thank you for the flowers baby, they were beautiful," I said not giving him a chance to respond and disappearing into the bathroom. I took a shower and got dressed in no time. I chose a simple burgundy bandage dress that I bought from Fashion Nova paired with a simple pair of black heels. It was sophisticated enough for me to wear to a business dinner but sexy enough to show off my curves and make me feel sexy. I let my hair down into a middle part with loose curls and applied a tad bit of make-up. Yasir had gone downstairs to watch some game before we left, so I made my way down there. Once he noticed me it was like his eyes lit up.

"Damn baby you look good as fuck. I'm happy as hell I'm about to show you off tonight," Yasir complimented and I blushed.

"Thank you, baby," I said pecking his lips. We left out of the house and made our way to the restaurant. We got to the restaurant, *Prime & Proper* and were immediately seated. I really just wanted to eat and go home and lay up with my man. Being fake happy to meet some strangers was not in my plans, but I'd do it for Yasir. I guess it wasn't too much to ask. He hasn't asked me for shit yet but this one thing. I was looking over the menu when I felt Yasir get up.

"Mr. James, how are you?" I heard him ask.

"I'm doing just fine Mr. White. Thank you again for inviting me," I heard a voice say and I almost peed on myself.

I knew that voice anywhere. I looked up from the menu and I immediately felt sick to my stomach. This could not be happening right now. No fucking way was Antonio Yasir's employee. Antonio couldn't be the outstanding employee with so much promise and potential that Yasir had been raving to me about for weeks. I tore my eyes away from him and looked at the obviously pregnant woman next to him in the tight navy blue off the shoulder dress. She couldn't have been more than a few months pregnant. Like a light bulb had just been turned on in my brain, I stood up.

"So, you cheated on me and got a bitch pregnant?" I spewed. Yasir looked at me like I had lost my mind.

"What?" he asked.

"He knows who I'm talking to," I said never taking my eyes off of Antonio. Instead of answering my question, he acted like everything was all good.

"How are you Lay Lay? You look beautiful, as you always do," he said smiling.

"What the fuck is going on?" Yasir asked slightly raising his voice.

"This is Talayah?" the pregnant girl asked. Finally, I looked at Yasir with tears in my eyes.

"Antonio is my ex-boyfriend," I told him, and I saw the vein in his head pop out. I looked down and noticed Yasir's hands balled up in a fist. Before anyone could say another word, Yasir hit Antonio with a mean right hook knocking him to the floor.

"Yasir no!!!!" I yelled.

TO BE CONTINUED…

Made in the USA
Columbia, SC
04 August 2023

21193013R00083